Spooksville

Three Books in One

Aliens in the Sky
The Cold People
The Witch's Revenge

Christopher Pike

Hodder
Children's
Books

a division of Hodder Headline plc

D1431634

A Catalogue record for this book is available
from the British Library

ISBN 0 340 72290 8

Typeset by Avon Dataset Ltd, Bidford-on-Avon, Warks

Printed and bound in Great Britain by
Mackays of Chatham, Chatham, Kent

Hodder Children's Books
a division of Hodder Headline plc
338 Euston Road
London NW1 3BH

Spooksville 4

ALIENS IN THE SKY

One

Spooksville seldom got real hot. Nestled between the hills beside the ocean, there was usually a cool breeze around the corner to prevent it from becoming uncomfortable, even in the middle of summer. But in the last half of July, only a couple of weeks after Adam and his friends had got trapped in the Haunted Cave, the temperature rose sharply. At midday, the thermometer burst past a hundred degrees. To get away from the heat, Sally suggested they head up to the reservoir.

'We won't go in the water,' she said. 'You don't want to do that. But it's always cooler up there.'

The four of them: Sally, Adam, Watch and Cindy were seated on Cindy's porch, drinking sodas and wiping their sweat-soaked brows. Adam stared at the half burnt-down lighthouse – about half a kilometre away – where earlier in the summer he had wrestled with a ghost. He felt like he was about to catch fire. He couldn't remember it ever having been so hot in Kansas City, which was known for its hot summers. He wondered what had brought the heat.

'Why can't you go in the water?' Cindy asked.

'Because you'll die,' Sally said simply.

'There are no fish in the reservoir,' Watch added. 'There's something unhealthy about the water.'

'But Spooksville gets its water from the reservoir,' Adam said.

'That's why so many children in town are born with deformities,' Sally said.

Cindy smiled. 'You were born here, Sally. That explains so much.'

'Not all deformities are bad,' Sally replied.

'The water is filtered before we drink it,' Watch said.

'What's filtered out?' Adam asked.

'I don't know,' Watch said. 'But it must be toxic stuff. The filtration plant has a habit of blowing up every couple of years.'

'Why is it cooler at the reservoir?' Adam asked.

Sally spoke. 'It's because Madeline Templeton – the witch who founded this city two hundred years ago – tortured fifty innocent people to death up there. The horror of that event reverberates psychically to this day, making the whole area cold as ice.'

Cindy made a face. 'And you want to go there to cool off?'

Sally shrugged. 'There is horror on almost any street in Spooksville, if you look deep enough into the past. Why, on this exact spot, where your house was built, Madeline Templeton once cut off a kid's head and fastened it on to a goat.'

'Yuck!' Cindy said. 'That's gross.'

'Yeah, but the kid was supposed to look like a goat anyway,' Watch said.

'Yeah,' Sally agreed. 'Maybe the witch did him a favour.'

'I don't know if she tortured the people to death at the reservoir,' Watch continued. 'I heard that she just made them go swimming in the water, and their skin turned grey and their hair all fell out.'

'I would rather die than lose my beautiful hair,' Sally said, brushing her brunette locks aside.

'I think the area is cooler because of all the subterranean streams that run under the ground,' Watch said, finally answering Adam's question. 'If you put your ear to the ground, you definitely hear gurgling water.'

Adam wiped away more sweat. 'Well, should we go there?'

Cindy was doubtful. 'The Haunted Cave is up there.'

'The Haunted Cave can't hurt you unless you're stupid

enough to go inside it,' Sally said.

'Thank you, Sally, for so gently reminding me of a past mistake,' Cindy said.

Sally spoke sweetly. 'Don't mention it, Cindy.'

'The Haunted Cave is located on a hill above the reservoir,' Watch said. 'We couldn't ride our bikes there last time, but if we're not climbing any rocky hills we can take them. We can get there in less than twenty minutes.' He tugged at his T-shirt, trying to cool off. 'I wouldn't mind hanging out there until it gets dark.'

'What do you think is causing this heat?' Adam asked.

'Could be an inversion layer,' Watch said.

'Or a curse from Ann Templeton,' Sally said. 'Madeline Templeton's seductive and evil descendant. She likes the heat. She likes all us kids to suffer in it.'

Adam shrugged. 'I'm for going.' He glanced at Cindy. 'If it's all right with you.'

Sally leant over and spoke in a *loud* whisper in Watch's ear. 'Notice how our dear Adam doesn't make a move without checking with his sweet Cindy.'

Cindy glared at Sally. 'He's just being polite. That's spelled P . . . O . . . L . . . I . . . T . . . E. Look it up in the dictionary. I know you've never heard of the word.' Cindy spoke to Adam. 'My mother doesn't care what I do, as long as I'm home before sunset.'

'My mother doesn't care what I do as long as I don't die,' Sally muttered.

Adam stood up. 'Then it's decided. We'll ride up there and stay until sunset.'

The others also stood up. Sally, as usual, wanted to have the last word.

'Let's leave before sunset,' she said. 'You never know what darkness might bring.'

Two

The bicycle ride up to the reservoir was harder than Adam had imagined. Because the place was in the hills behind Spooksville, they had to pedal on an incline most of the way. But it was the temperature that really stole Adam's strength. He was feeling wobbly when they arrived at the water and climbed off their bikes. Fortunately, they had each brought large plastic bottles of water.

'I feel a lot cooler now,' Adam said, sarcastically, as he opened his bottle and held it up to his lips. 'Now that we're here.'

'It's like being in an air-conditioned mall,' Cindy agreed, also reaching for her water bottle. Her face was red from the sun and the exertion.

'It actually is cooler here,' Watch said, stepping to the edge of the reservoir, which was a rough oval, maybe half a kilometre long, half that in width. The water was a strange grey colour. The surrounding bank was almost entirely devoid of trees. Their words seemed to die in the air the instant they left their mouths. Watch continued, 'It's got to be at least ten degrees cooler.'

'I feel refreshed from our ride,' Sally said, although she had already plopped down on a boulder and drained half her water bottle. 'I think my suggestion was a good one.'

Cindy had brought a bag of sandwiches. Finding shade beneath one of the few trees, they sat down and ate their food. As they munched and talked and drank, Adam did begin to feel a lot cooler. They had set off for the reservoir after four. It was now half past five, and the sun was just beginning to ease up on them. But it was still too hot to do much exploring, not that any of them were in the mood to try another local cave.

Watch happened to have a pack of cards on him, and wanted to play poker. Apparently Watch and Sally often played together. Adam was curious although he had never played the game before and didn't know the rules. But Cindy was uneasy.

'My mother doesn't approve of gambling,' Cindy said. 'She says it's immoral and disgusting.'

'Those two words fit me nicely,' Sally said jokingly. 'Listen, we're just going to gamble with smooth pebbles. We start with twenty each. It's not real gambling unless

8

you have real money at stake. I mean, how can your mother be upset if you lose a pile of rocks?'

Cindy chuckled. 'You have a point there. All right, I will play as long as I don't have to wager my next week's allowance.'

Watch explained the rules of five card stud and for the next hour they played many hands. But Watch and Sally were way ahead of Adam and Cindy when it came to the subtleties of the game. Adam and Cindy quickly lost all their pebbles, and even fierce Sally was steadily withering under Watch's apparent skill. She got down to five pebbles, but finally seemed to be holding a strong hand because she bet two of them at once. Watch was unmoved; he matched her bet.

'I think you're bluffing,' he said confidently.

Sally caught his eye. 'You think so, babe.' She picked up the remainder of her pebbles. 'I raise you another three. Count them – seven grand on the table at once.'

Watch was unimpressed. 'I still think you're bluffing.'

Sally sneered. 'Thoughts aren't rocks. Put your pebbles where your mouth is.'

Coolly Watch matched her bet. 'There's ten grand on the table now.'

Sally was momentarily taken back. 'I can't believe you did that.'

9

'What have you got?' Watch asked.

Sally threw her cards down. 'Trash. You win. Darn.'

'It was an impressive bluff,' Adam told Sally.

'I fell for it,' Cindy agreed.

'It's not impressive unless it works,' Sally muttered.

The sun was getting near the horizon and they were thinking of returning home when a minor disaster struck. Cindy, who was still curious about the Haunted Cave, had hiked up to peek at the opening, just to see if it was closed or what. The others had allowed her to go by herself because she had promised not to step inside if it was open. She was on her way back down the hill, looking excited, when she must have stepped on some loose gravel. The ground seemed to go out from under her, and then she was toppling.

'Cindy!' Adam shouted. Sally and Watch looked over, and soon all three were running to Cindy's aid. In reality she had not toppled far, maybe five metres. But it was enough to pick up several scrapes and bruises. She was wearing shorts; her legs were bleeding slightly in a few places. But that was not the major problem. As they reached her, they saw her clutching her right ankle. Adam knelt by her side.

'Did you twist it?' he asked.

Cindy grimaced. 'Yeah. It hurts.'

'You didn't break it, did you?' Sally asked, concerned. 'Your bones are not sticking out, are they?'

'If you did break it, there's going to be no ambulance coming to your aid,' Watch said matter-of-factly. 'Spooksville's ambulance drivers have all long since disappeared.'

'Would you two shut up?' Adam said. 'Can't you see she's in pain?'

Cindy forced a smile. 'It's not too bad. I want to try putting some weight on it.'

'You might want to ice it first,' Watch suggested.

'Like we just happen to have bags of ice with us,' Sally said sarcastically.

Adam helped Cindy up. The moment Cindy put her right foot down, she let out a soft cry. 'Ah,' she said, breathing heavily. 'It really is sore.'

Adam pointed to the reservoir. 'Maybe you should soak it in the water. It will help with the swelling.'

'I wouldn't put my foot in that water if you'd just splashed sulphuric acid on my toes,' Sally said.

Watch strolled over to the water and crouched down. Before any of them could say a word, he reached over and cupped a handful of water. He raised it to his lips and swallowed, then nodded, satisfied.

'It could use a little fluoride, but otherwise it tastes fine,' he said.

'We should wait a minute and see if he falls over dead,' Sally whispered to Adam and Cindy.

Watch walked back to them. 'I don't think it will melt your skin off, Cindy. But put your whole foot in the water with your shoe still on. The pressure of the sides of the shoe will help the swelling as much as the cold water.'

'OK,' Cindy muttered, as Watch and Adam moved to either side and helped her to a spot where the water and ground met. She sat down, 'I feel like such a clutz, falling like that.'

'I fell,' Sally said proudly. 'Once. But I regained my balance before causing myself any harm.'

'Was the Haunted Cave open or closed?' Watch asked.

'It's still closed,' Cindy replied, as she carefully placed her aching ankle into the water. 'I didn't have the nerve to try to open it with one of the magic words we learned from the witch.' She twitched. 'Hey, this water is really cold.'

'Some people say the reservoir is bottomless,' Sally said. 'Certainly none of the bodies dumped here over the years have ever floated back to the surface.'

'I think I'm going to talk my parents into buying a water purifier when I get home,' Adam said. He clasped Cindy's hand and spoke in a gentle voice. 'Is the pain becoming less?'

'Oh, Watch,' Sally said, touching her heart. 'Look at his bedside manner. He's a born doctor. Dr Adam – he sounds like he could be a brain surgeon.'

'It feels better, thank you,' Cindy said, ignoring Sally. 'If I can just soak it for a few minutes, maybe I'll be able to ride back home.'

'You can ride a bike with one foot,' Sally said. 'Jaws does it all the time.'

'That's the kid who lost a leg to the great white shark who stays off our coast,' Watch reminded them.

'You're lucky there are no sharks in the reservoir,' Sally added.

'We'll wait here until you feel strong enough to travel,' Adam told Cindy.

Watch nodded toward the west. 'The sun is setting. It will be dark soon.'

'This is just what I was afraid would happen,' Sally said. She took a step away from the water and sat back down. 'There's no moon tonight. It will get black as ink up here.'

Three

Watch and Sally were both right. Not long after the sun left, the stars started to come out. As the night deepened, the numbers rose dramatically. Adam had never seen so many stars, nor had he ever enjoyed the Milky Way before. The faint nebulous river of the galaxy stretched across the entire sky. Watch, who seemed to know a great deal about astronomy, pointed out the Northern Cross and told them about the blue white star at the base of it.

'That's Deneb,' he said. 'It's tens of thousands of times brighter than our sun. I think it's the brightest star in the sky that we can see. It has a red star that circles it, but you can't see it with the naked eye.'

'But what about that one?' Sally asked, pointing straight overhead. 'That's several times brighter.'

'That's Vega,' Watch said. 'It's twenty-six light years away. It's also a lot brighter than our sun. But it's no

Deneb. Deneb is thousands of times further away than Vega. If Deneb was only twenty-six light years from here, it would dominate the whole sky.'

'How did you learn all these things?' Cindy asked, impressed.

In the dark, Watch shrugged. They could hardly see each other. Each of them was just a black line, drawn against the stars.

'I have a telescope at home,' Watch said. 'And I study the books on astronomy at the library. Mr Spiney has a few good ones.'

'Watch built his own telescope,' Sally said, with a trace of pride in her voice.

They were enjoying the stars, and listening to Watch's stories about the constellations so much, they hardly noticed the passage of time. Cindy had been soaking her foot for close to an hour when Adam suggested that she try putting weight on it again. They helped her up, and she gently put her foot down. She was about to tell them how it felt, but something remarkable interrupted her.

A strange light appeared in the sky.

'What the heck is that?' Sally gasped.

Straight overhead was a white light, much brighter than any star. At first it was just a point; they could not tell its size. But as they watched, it grew brighter, and they all received the impression that it was coming towards them. Just then it stopped, hovering far above.

'Is it a plane?' Cindy whispered.

'A helicopter can hover,' Watch said. 'Not a plane. But I don't think it's a helicopter. We should be able to hear its rotary blades.'

'Could it be a balloon?' Adam asked.

'It's not moving like a balloon,' Watch said. 'It swept down and then just stopped.'

Sally chuckled uneasily. 'Well, it's not a flying saucer, is it?'

There was a moment of silence.

'That's exactly what I think it is,' Watch said finally.

'We should get out of here,' Cindy said.

'I don't know,' Adam said, getting excited. 'I've always wanted to see a UFO. Do you think it will land, Watch?'

Watch shrugged. 'This is Spooksville. Where else on Earth could an alien feel so at home?'

Perhaps the occupants aboard the strange light heard Watch. For at that moment it began to descend once more, dropping like a glowing meteorite out of a black abyss. They realised that they were staring at two vessels, not one. The ships had been flying so close together that their light had blurred. Adam's excitement was blunted by an edge of fear. The lights changed from white glows to definite shapes. They were definitely flying saucers – and they were coming down fast.

They clearly intended to land at the reservoir.

'Maybe we should go hide behind the rocks,' Adam said quickly. 'At least at first.'

Watch considered for one second. 'Good idea. Can you walk, Cindy?'

'I can hobble if you guys help me,' she replied, fear in her voice. The saucers were now only half a kilometre overhead. Their brilliant white glow radiated out over the surface of the reservoir, turning it into one huge silver mirror. For a moment they halted again, apparently searching for a place to set down. Unfortunately the ships made up their minds swiftly.

The UFOs wanted to park beside their bikes.

'Let's carry her!' Adam shouted, as they stumbled slowly towards the large rocks, behind which they hoped to hide.

'Good idea!' Watch shouted back.

They didn't even ask Cindy for permission. They just each grabbed a leg and yanked her up so that she was riding above their shoulders. Sally ran ahead of them, leaping on to the rocks. She was clearly visible, they all were. Behind them, the saucers hovered five metres above their bicycles. Incredibly, there was no noise, not even a faint hum.

'I hope they didn't see us,' Adam gasped, as they carried

Cindy around the largest boulder and set her down. Above their heads, the glow stabbed past the edges of the rocks. Certain that Cindy was sitting comfortably, Adam, Sally and Watch climbed back up the boulders and peered over the edge.

Both ships had set down beside the water, practically on top of their bicycles. One continued to glow brilliantly. The other seemed to have turned off its engine or warp drive or whatever. It gave off a feeble white glow, nothing more. Both ships were saucer-shaped, circular, maybe ten metres in diameter. Actually, they looked like saucers with cups placed on top. It didn't take a genius to know they were not from planet Earth.

'What's happening?' Cindy whispered, below them.

'They're unloading an antimatter bomb and preparing to blow up the planet,' Sally said.

'Quiet,' Adam cautioned. 'They're just sitting there. Nothing's . . . Wait! I think I see a door opening.'

Adam was right. On the ship that was no longer glowing brightly, a door of sorts was materialising. It was a peculiar opening. There had been no sign of it a few seconds ago. It was as if the walls of the ship had suddenly dissolved in a rectangular pattern. Yellow light shone from inside. The door was not large; Adam would have had to stoop to enter the vessel.

'Do you see any aliens?' Adam asked.

'I'm the last person to ask,' Watch said. 'I'm half blind.'

'I hope they're not disgusting looking,' Sally whispered. 'Even E.T. gave me nightmares.'

'You can't think that way,' Watch said. 'They have probably travelled millions of miles to get here. They will have evolved from an entirely separate genetic tree. We will probably look horrible to them.'

'I think I look horrible to my own mother half the time,' Sally muttered.

'Shh,' Adam cautioned. 'One of them is coming out.'

Four

Actually, there were two of them coming out of the flying saucer. They could not have looked more alien. Their skin was vaguely scaly, brown; their heads were huge relative to their tiny bodies. Their faces were shaped in V's. Although their mouths and noses were tiny, their eyes were large, black, almond-shaped. Their legs and arms were bony, but they had big hands, and what looked like only four fingers, no thumb. They wore thin tan jump-suits, a black belt that carried exotic tools. In their hands they appeared to carry weapons of some kind. As they stepped from their ship they both searched around, very alert.

'What's happening?' Cindy said from below.

'They're as disgusting as I imagined they would be,' Sally whispered.

'But they look friendly,' Watch said.

'Watch!' Sally hissed. 'They're carrying weapons.'

'Probably only for protection,' Watch said.

'Yeah, right,' Sally said. 'I bet they shoot first and ask questions later.'

Watch shook his head. 'They are obviously from a culture far more advanced than our own. I am sure they have left mindless violence far behind. I want to talk to them.'

'I don't know,' Adam said quietly. 'Their technology may be advanced, but that does not mean they will be friendly. For all we know, they could be here to collect specimens. Watch, you've talked about that before. We might be better to stay out of sight, and just see what happens. Oh, look, the other ship's light has gone off. I think I see another door forming.'

The second ship was also opening up. Another two aliens stepped from the saucer. They joined their buddies, who now stood by the water, beside their bicycles. The aliens gestured with their instruments at the bikes. They seemed to be carrying on a conversation but they were not talking, or making any other kind of sound. Watch had an explanation.

'They probably communicate using telepathy,' Watch said. 'Exchanging thoughts directly from mind to mind.'

'Do you think they can read our minds from here?' Sally asked, worried.

'Who knows?' Watch said. 'But I still want to make contact with them.'

'Why?' Adam asked. 'I think it's too risky.'

Watch shrugged. 'I want to go for a ride in one of their spaceships.' He moved to leave them. 'You guys can stay here.'

Sally grabbed his arm. 'Wait a second. They can see there are four bikes. They'll come looking for us, if they like the look of you, or even if they don't like your look. You're risking all of us with this mad idea.'

Watch spoke seriously. 'Why do we live in Spooksville? It's not just because our families live here. It's because this is a place of adventure. The unknown surrounds us every time we leave our homes. I know what I'm doing is dangerous. All great adventures are.'

Cindy was impressed. 'That was a nice speech, Watch.'

'If they capture you, and take you prisoner,' Adam said, 'I don't know if we'll be able to rescue you.' He gripped his friend's hand. 'If they take you inside their ship, we may never see you again.'

There was still a faint glow from the saucers. They could see Watch's face just enough to read his expression. For a moment he seemed touched, an unusual emotion for him.

Most of the time Watch showed as much emotion as, well, one of the aliens hanging out by the water.

'You would miss me?' he asked, surprised.

'We would miss you terribly, you major idiot,' Sally said.

'Be careful,' Cindy called out from below. 'Don't take any unnecessary risks.'

'The only way you can do that in this town is to stay in bed twenty-four hours a day,' Sally said. But she reached over and gave Watch a hug. 'Don't let them do any genetic experiments on you. You're fine the way you are, really.'

Adam shook Watch's hand. 'Shout for help if you think you're in trouble.'

'Just don't use our names,' Sally added.

Watch said goodbye and slowly walked down towards the reservoir. As soon as he was away from the rocks, the aliens looked over and raised what appeared to be their weapons. From the reaction of the aliens, it did not appear as if they knew Watch – and therefore the rest of them – had been there to begin with. Adam said as much to Sally and Cindy, who had now crawled up to the edge of the rocks so that she could see.

'That's probably true,' Sally said. 'But why is such an advanced race greeting Watch with pointed weapons?'

Adam was grim. 'Especially when he's holding out his

hands to show he's not armed. I don't like this.'

'He's such a brave boy,' Cindy whispered, anxious.

'He's a fool,' Sally remarked. 'A brave fool.'

The aliens may or may not have tried to communicate with Watch. From a distance of fifty metres it was hard to tell. It did appear as if Watch tried to talk to them, but Adam and his friends could not hear the telepathic thoughts the aliens may have responded with. However, the aliens certainly did not lower their weapons. Finally, after a couple of minutes of inspecting Watch from all angles, one of the aliens grabbed his arm and led him towards the door of the first saucer. Although Watch did not put up a fight, his friends got the impression he was being dragged into the ship. Sally and Adam and Cindy looked at each other anxiously.

'What are we going to do now?' Cindy asked.

'Well,' Sally said. 'He wanted to see the ship. Now he gets to see the ship.'

'He wants to go for a joy-ride in space,' Adam countered. 'He doesn't want to be dissected.' Adam shook his head. 'We can't just sit here and do nothing.'

'I have a bad feeling that we can do nothing against their ray-guns,' Sally said. 'Maybe we should call the President of the United States.'

'It will take us forever to reach a phone,' Adam said.

'We have to save Watch ourselves.' He went to get up. 'I'm going to speak to the aliens.'

Sally grabbed his arm and pulled him back down. 'You think you're going to have more success than Watch? Can't you see what's going on here? These aliens are here to collect genetic material to microscopically implant in their DNA to enrich and regenerate their ancient and failing species.'

'You can tell all that just by looking at them?' Cindy asked doubtfully.

Adam shook free of Sally. 'I don't want to walk out there any more than you want to. If you have a better plan, let's hear it.'

Sally thought for a moment. 'Nothing comes to me right away. But let's not act hastily. Let's wait and see what happens.'

What happened next as far as Watch was concerned was nothing. He did not reappear. But two of the aliens left the area around the reservoir and hiked back into the hills, not far from where Adam and his friends were crouched.

'They could be trying to encircle us,' Sally said.

Adam nodded darkly. 'We have to keep an eye on our backs. But if I am going to confront them, this might be the time, while they're at half strength.'

'I can't let you go out there alone,' Sally said.

'You can't come with me,' Adam said. 'Cindy's injured. Someone has to stay with her.'

'I'd rather you didn't go down there alone,' Cindy said. 'Take Sally with you.'

'I wasn't volunteering myself,' Sally complained. 'I was just speaking generally.' She paused and frowned. 'I suppose I could go with you, Adam. But I hate us not having a plan of action. We'll probably be taken prisoner like Watch and dragged to a distant planet circling a dying sun where we'll be dumped in a sterile prison and sliced open with a burning laser beam. Why, we're lambs going to slaughter.'

'You're not a lamb, Sally,' Cindy said.

'I was speaking poetically,' Sally said.

'Tell me what else to do,' Adam said.

'I don't know what else to do,' Sally snapped back. 'I just know that you can't trust gross-looking aliens with hand phasers.'

'They only have phasers on *Star Trek*,' Cindy said.

'How do we know these guys didn't write the TV show?' Sally asked.

Adam spoke wearily. 'We're getting nowhere with this arguing. I'm going down to demand that they release Watch. You can come if you want, Sally. But I don't think it's a good idea.'

'You mean it's all right for you to be a hero and not me?' Sally asked, getting to her feet. 'Really, Adam, you're a bit of a sexist. A girl can save the day just as easily as a boy.' She glanced at the saucers again. Only one alien stood visible, near the door of the first ship, the door through which Watch had disappeared. 'I wonder if there are boy aliens and girl aliens.'

'Right now I think that's the least of our worries,' Adam said.

'You never know,' Sally replied. She leaned over and patted Cindy on the back. 'If we don't come back, and you do manage to escape, write a book about me when you grow up. The world has to know what it lost tonight.'

Cindy was not in a joking mood. 'I wish you guys plenty of luck.'

Together, Adam and Sally crept from behind the rocks and walked slowly in the direction of the two saucers. The alien standing guard reacted quickly to their approach. Stepping towards them, he drew his weapon and pointed it at their heads. Adam and Sally put up their arms. Up close, the alien looked even more strange. It had no nails on its fingers, and not a trace of hair on its body. Its huge black eyes were completely devoid of emotion or feeling. They were so cold they could have belonged to an insect. Adam felt a sinking feeling in his chest. He doubted he would be able to reason with the creature.

'Hello,' Adam said. 'We come in peace. We mean you no harm. My name is Adam. This is my friend, Sally. Inside your flying saucer you have another friend of ours named Watch. We just want him back. That is all we want.'

'But we do have friends in high places,' Sally added. 'And they would avenge our deaths with great relish.'

'Shh,' Adam cautioned her. 'I don't know if it understands us.'

The alien just stared at them for a minute. Then it gestured with its weapon. It wanted them to walk into the flying saucer. Adam shook his head.

'No,' Adam said. 'We want our friend back. We don't want to go in your ship. Give him back to us and we won't bother you any more.'

'Yeah,' Sally added. 'And remember that you're a visitor to this planet. Show some manners, would ya?'

Apparently the alien didn't like Sally's tone. It took a step forward and grabbed her right arm. She shook it off – it did not appear that strong – but immediately it grabbed her again and pointed its weapon directly between her eyes. Sally recoiled in terror. That was enough for Adam. He was through talking. No more Mr Nice Human.

Adam launched himself at the alien.

The alien spun on him. Levelled its weapon.

Adam saw a flash of green light. Heard Sally scream.

Then everything went black.

Five

For Cindy, watching Adam and Sally fight with the alien was the hardest thing she had ever done. Cindy knew from the start the battle was hopeless. It especially hurt that she could do nothing to help the others. A second after the alien shot Adam, it turned its weapon on Sally. To her credit, Sally did not turn and run. She tried to attack the alien. But the creature was too quick for her. The black instrument in its hand spurted another blast of green light, and Sally collapsed on the ground beside Adam.

Cindy didn't even know if either of them were still alive.

She was not given long to grieve over her fallen pals. Behind her she heard sounds further up the hill. The other two aliens were either returning to their ship or else closing in to take her captive. Sprained ankle or not, Cindy swore to herself she would not be taken without a fight.

Climbing to her feet, hobbling on one foot, she listened closer, trying to determine the course of the aliens. They did not appear to be coming directly towards her. Instead they were following the path of a narrow valley that cut through the side of the hill where she was hiding. Actually, it was more of a ravine, cut by the winter rains. It was only thirty metres to her right. Cindy decided she would hide above the lip of the ravine and shower rocks down on the aliens as they came by. If she could get a hold of just one of their weapons, she thought, it would help even out the fight.

Trying her best to move silently, Cindy half hopped and half dragged herself to the edge of the ravine. She got there none too soon. The two aliens were almost directly below her. Grabbing hold of a watermelon-sized rock, she lifted it over her head. There was faint background light coming from the two saucers, although both ships were in dim mode. It helped her to aim, but here in the ravine it was poor shooting at best. As she let fly the first rock, she thought she would need a miracle to hit anything.

There was a flash of green light.

Cindy blinked. Had she been shot?

No. Quite the reverse.

Below her, the two aliens lay unconscious on the ground.

'But who shot them?' Cindy whispered aloud. Looking around, she couldn't find another soul, human or alien. Briefly she wondered if she had imagined the green light. Or maybe her rock had hit them, after all – both of them. Or perhaps one of their weapons had accidentally gone off when they struck the ground. It didn't really matter, she decided. She was taking their weapons now. She had fought with ghosts and hyeets. She could handle aliens.

Cindy hobbled down to where the aliens lay silent. They appeared stunned, not dead. She could hear them breathing. Quickly she stripped off their black belts, tucking one gun in her own belt while keeping the other ready in her right hand. She didn't know how these particular guns were set, if they would stun or kill when she fired them. But fire them she would, as soon as she got sight of that monster who'd shot Adam and Sally.

Cindy hobbled back to her position behind the rocks. But here there was no chance for her to rest. The alien and his partner were dragging Adam into the saucer. They could not be very strong. Even though there were two of them, they were struggling with Adam's lifeless body. But Cindy had no doubt they would come back for Sally in a minute. Unfortunately for Adam, they were already beside the saucer.

Cindy had a moment of panic. The ship was fifty metres away. She could not run there; she could hardly walk. On the other hand, she could not simply stand and start shooting, not without the risk of hitting Adam. But she had to do something and she had to do it now. People who went into that ship did not come out.

Cindy took aim. But not directly at the aliens. She aimed for the saucer itself. Pulling the trigger, she felt no recoil but saw a narrow flash of green light. It hit the side of the craft, and made the aliens jump. For a moment they dropped Adam and pointed in her direction. They raised their own weapons. For an instant, Cindy wondered if they took target practice in their home world – and whether their weapons were set to kill.

The large rock beside her exploded.

Cindy dived for cover. But after crawling a few feet to the side, she was back up again in a moment. So they wanted to play rough. Cindy twisted a tiny knob on her weapon all the way round in the other direction. Of course she did not know what the knob controlled, but she figured it might boost the weapon's power. Again she took aim at the saucer and pulled the trigger.

Her ray-gun was no longer set on stun.

The ship exploded with sparks as the green beam licked its surface. However, the hull of the saucer did not break. The ship was probably still capable of spaceflight. Cindy fired again, and got a similar violent response. But she was having to be very careful not to aim at the aliens or Adam, who were terribly exposed. At least she had a ton of rocks to hide behind. They took another couple of shots at her and set a bunch of dust flying, but they didn't even come close to hitting her. They appeared anxious to get inside and get away. Maybe they were not used to humans who fought back.

Grabbing Adam, they pulled him into the saucer.

Before Cindy could get off a third shot, the door vanished.

'No!' Cindy screamed, and jumped out from her place behind the rocks, almost falling over with her bad ankle. The saucer began to glow brightly. She knew it was preparing for take off. Raising her weapon once more, she took aim. This time she fired off a series of shots in quick succession. The saucer shook under the pounding, and smoke and sparks were everywhere. But Cindy should have realised that the saucer had weapons of its own. As it bobbled off the ground, it spun round and Cindy saw two green streaks rush along the perimeter of the ship towards each other. As they collided, a blinding beam of light flashed in her direction. Instinctively, Cindy dived to the side and half the hill behind her seemed to fly into the air in one gigantic explosion.

The noise was deafening, the shock wave crushing. If Cindy had not been flat on the ground, she surely would have been killed. As it was, she lay stunned for several moments, recovering only when the saucer was a vanishing white dot in the sky. She opened her eyes just as it blinked out of view.

'They got Adam,' she whispered. 'They got Watch.'

But they had not got Sally. Cindy found her lying unmoving, not far from the remaining saucer. Smoke and tiny fires littered the landscape. Sally had a pulse, she was breathing. Cindy hobbled to the water and soaked her own shirt in it. Then she returned to Sally and squeezed the water on to her friend's face. Sally opened her eyes with a start.

'That'd better not be water from the reservoir,' Sally said.

'It is,' Cindy said.

Sally sat up and wiped her face with the back of her arm. 'You'd better pray my face doesn't turn grey and my hair doesn't fall out,' she complained. 'Or else you're going to be bobbing for apples tomorrow night in a barrel of reservoir water.'

'They've taken Adam and Watch,' Cindy cried.

'Oh, my head hurts.' Sally rubbed her forehead. 'What are you talking about?'

'The aliens! Their ship left with them in it!'

Sally was instantly alert. She glanced around. 'Why didn't they take me?'

Cindy held up one of her weapons. 'I ambushed a couple of aliens and took their guns. They're lying over there in the ravine, unconscious.' Cindy paused and gestured to the remaining flying saucer. 'Why don't we drag them back to their own ship, wake them up and put a gun to their heads and demand that they go after Adam and Watch?'

Sally thought for a moment and smiled wickedly.

'Sounds like my kind of plan,' she said.

Six

When Adam came to, he was lying on his back. The first thing he felt – besides the floor beneath him – was his splitting headache. He could hear his pulse in his head. It pounded like thunder. Every time his heart beat, it was as if the nerves in his brain squeezed together. He felt so awful he saw no point in even opening his eyes. But he did anyway.

'How are you doing?' Watch asked, sitting beside him. 'Got a headache?'

Adam groaned. 'Yeah. How did you know?'

'I had the same thing when I woke up. I felt like my skull was about to explode. I think I got zapped by the same gun as you.'

Right then Adam remembered the alien and his nasty weapon. He pulled himself into an upright position. It took a moment before his vision settled down enough that he could see straight. Immediately he thought he was imagining things.

He was inside an alien craft flying through space. The ship was not large. It was only about five metres from where he and Watch sat to the other side where the two aliens stood at an exotic control panel. Except for the controls, the interior was relatively featureless and rather dim. Adam had to squint to see clearly. The floor was a simple tan carpet. The walls were black and off-white in colour. The aliens had obviously not hired an interior decorator when they were building their ship. Every ninety degrees, on the side walls, was a small circular viewing screen.

But overhead was a glorious sight. The ceiling appeared to be one huge viewing portal. Adam had thought he had seen a lot of stars, sitting beside the reservoir. There had to be a hundred times that number now. The Milky Way seemed to shimmer with magical radiance. The unblinking stars looked close enough to touch. He wondered if they had already left the solar system. Watch shook his head.

'This ship changes orientation every few minutes,' he said. 'Not long ago I saw the sun through the ceiling. It's a lot smaller in size than seen from Earth but at least it's still there.'

'Do you know where we're headed?'

'Your guess is as good as mine. But I would assume we're returning to the aliens' home world.'

'Do you think it's in our solar system?' Adam asked.

'No. There isn't another planet in our solar system that can support life. It has to be around another star. It may not even be in our galaxy.'

'Great. What will we do there?' Adam said.

Watch shrugged. 'I try not to think about it.'

Adam nodded to the two aliens, who appeared to be ignoring them for the time being. 'Have they spoken to you?'

'No. They act as if I'm not even here. But I'm convinced they're telepathic. They communicate strictly in silence.'

'Do you think they can read our minds?' Adam asked.

'I'm not sure. If they can, I think they have to concentrate on us to pick up our thoughts. That's just an impression I get.'

Adam gestured to the absence of chains. 'How come they haven't tied us up?'

'We don't exactly have a lot of places we can run to.'

'You have a point there,' Adam agreed.

'Also, I think one blast of their guns was enough to let us know who's in charge. Is your head feeling any better?'

Adam rubbed his neck. 'Yeah, it's getting there.'

'The pain goes away pretty quickly, once you're awake.'

Adam remembered something. 'You know, just before I was shot, one of the aliens was wrestling with Sally. I wonder how she got away.'

'Maybe she didn't. Maybe she's aboard the other ship.'

'Have you seen it?' Adam asked.

'No. But I assume it isn't far behind us.'

Adam lowered his voice. 'Do you have an escape plan?'

'No.'

'You must have some ideas?'

Watch shook his head. 'Neither of us knows how to pilot this ship. We can't forcibly take over, even if they give us half a chance. We're stuck.'

'But I don't want to live the rest of my life on an alien planet.'

'The rest of your life might not be that long.'

'You're encouraging,' Adam complained.

'I'm sorry. I just can't imagine how we're going to get out of this. Unless the aliens decide to take us home. And I don't think that's likely. Not after they went to so much trouble to kidnap us.'

'Did they stun you as soon as you went in the ship?'

'No. Only when I tried to leave.' Watch nodded as if impressed. 'They've got pretty cool guns. I wonder what scientific principle they use.'

Just then a circular door appeared in the centre of the

42

floor, and a small alien, riding a narrow lift, appeared. He looked like a kid, although as far as Adam knew he might be ten thousand years old. Like the others, he had a huge head, even though his big black eyes did not seem as cold. He stared at them for a moment and then walked over. He seemed to bow slightly as he stopped near their feet. He couldn't have been half a metre tall.

'Hello,' Adam said flatly. 'What's your name? Or do you just have a number?'

To Adam's immense surprise, a reply immediately formed in his mind. It was not a thought of his own. The texture and clarity of it was much sharper. It was almost as if a miniature being had crawled inside his brain and shouted something aloud. The unspoken words definitely came from the creature in front of them.

'*My name is a combination of syllables and numbers. I am Ekwee12. Who are you?*'

Adam had to take a deep breath. The reply had startled him, yet also pleased him. He had not been looking forward to spending the rest of his days with mute aliens.

'I'm Adam, and this is my friend Watch.'

The alien continued to stare at him with his big eyes. His face showed no emotion. '*What is your number?*'

'We don't have numbers where we come from,' Adam said.

'What is your rating then?'

'We don't have ratings either,' Adam added. 'But I will be in seventh grade next year. Hopefully.'

'I don't think they have junior high where we're heading,' Watch muttered.

The alien glanced at Watch. 'What is junior high?'

'It's a type of school,' Adam said. 'It means you're too old to play with toys, but not old enough to drive a car.'

'What is a car? A vehicle of transportation?'

'Yes,' Adam said. 'We have them on our planet.' He nodded to the other two aliens, who continued to ignore them. 'How are you related to those two guys?'

'They are teachers. This is an educational trip for me.'

Adam spoke bitterly. 'Are they teaching you to kidnap innocent people?'

The alien hesitated. For a moment the skin around his mouth seemed to wrinkle. He glanced at the aliens behind him and then back at them.

'Explain the word kidnap?'

'It means we have been taken against our will,' Adam said. 'Your teachers knocked us out with their weapons. I was dragged unconscious aboard this ship. Didn't you see any of this happen?'

Again the alien paused. He seemed to be thinking.

'No. I was told to stay below after we landed.'

'But you believe our story, don't you?' Adam asked, for he sensed that the little alien did not approve of what had been done. Once more the alien took a moment before answering.

'*You do not appear to be lying.*'

'We're telling you what happened,' Watch said. 'We were attacked by your people.'

'*You are not hurt.*'

'But we are held captive,' Watch said. 'We want to go home.'

'*We are going home.*'

'We want to go to *our* home,' Adam said. 'Back to where we were picked up.' He paused. 'Can you help us?'

The little alien lowered his head. '*I am just a student. I am not in charge here.*'

'But maybe you could talk to your teachers,' Adam said. 'Explain to them that we are upset.'

The little alien glanced over his shoulder. '*They would not listen.*'

Adam was curious. 'Are they listening to us now?'

The little alien closed his eyes briefly. It was the first time they had seen his eyelids. They were faintly translucent, pretty weird-looking. When he opened his eyes again, Adam thought he saw a faint spark in those black depths.

'No. They are not listening. They do not care about you two. Also, among my people, the young are better telepaths. My telepathic range is twice theirs.'

'That's interesting,' Adam said. 'I thought it would have been the other way around. Why are kids better at picking up and sending thought?'

'We have less stress.'

'We seem to be picking up speed,' Watch said. 'But even going this fast, I don't see how we're going to reach your home planet in the next century. Can you explain how this craft works?'

'This ship first accelerates to near light speed. Then we convert our momentum to pure energy and use the power to jump through hyperspace. We can only make such a jump far from the gravitational pull of the Sun.'

'Can we cross many light years in a single hyperjump?' Watch asked.

The alien hesitated as if for once he did not understand the question. 'Yes. We can travel any distance, if it is necessary.'

'What does all this mean?' Adam asked Watch.

'That we're in serious trouble,' Watch replied. 'If we don't reverse our course before the hyperjump, I doubt we'll ever get home.'

'When do we jump through hyperspace?' Adam asked the little alien.

The alien consulted a small instrument fastened to his wrist. *'Fifteen of your minutes.'*

Adam was aghast. 'That's so soon.' He tried to keep his voice steady, yet he spoke with passion. 'Do you care about us? Can you help us escape?'

The little alien may have tried to smile then. Once more the tan flesh around his tiny narrow mouth creased. He probably shouldn't have bothered. His expression looked anything but friendly. But Adam sensed his good intentions.

'I care that your free will may have been violated. That is against the laws of our people. I do not understand how our teachers could have committed such a violation.'

'You should point that out to them,' Watch suggested.

But the alien repeated his earlier comment. *'They would not listen.'*

Adam was sympathetic. 'Adults don't listen to kids in your world either? It's the same where we come from. We have plenty of smart things to say but we're not even allowed to vote for who is president of our country.' Adam paused. He spoke in a whisper. 'Do you know how to fly this ship?'

'Yes.'

'Can you help us escape?' Adam asked again, not wanting to push the guy but worried about the coming hyperjump. 'We really have to get home. My mother's already made me dinner by now. She'll be wondering where I am.'

The little alien seemed to understand.

'I have a mother as well. She is nice to me.' The alien glanced once more at the others. He seemed lost in thought, or perhaps even in confusion. He sent them a final mental communication. *'I will have to consider the situation.'*

The alien turned and stepped to where the others stood. They acknowledged his arrival with a slight nod of their two fat heads, but if they communicated with the little guy Adam and Watch did not hear it, with their ears or their minds. Adam continued to fret about the hyperjump.

'What do you know about hyperspace?' he asked Watch.

Watch shrugged. 'Our scientists only have theories that it even exists. But it sounds like this ship is capable of sliding into a short cut through space. That's what hyperspace must be. This ship uses the energy of its tremendous speed to open the door to the short cut.'

'Then we have to brake somehow,' Adam said.

'You can throw one of your shoes at the control panel, but I don't think that will do the trick,' Watch said. 'It will probably just get you shot again. And this time they might not have their guns on stun.'

Adam went to stand. 'I'm tired of just sitting here doing

nothing. I'd rather go down fighting.'

Watch grabbed his arm. 'We have to be patient. The little guy clearly wants to help us. Let's give him a chance.'

Reluctantly Adam sat down again. 'I'll give him ten minutes, that's all.'

But he didn't have to wait that long. Five minutes later, the other flying saucer suddenly appeared. They saw it through the transparent ceiling. It swooped dangerously close, glowing brightly, and as it did an angry burst of green light struck the ceiling. For a moment, Adam and Watch were blinded. Their own flying saucer shook violently as the lights dimmed further. Adam thought he smelt smoke.

The two aliens at the controls gestured excitably, although they didn't say a word. They probably could speak if they wanted to. They had radio communication – Adam and Watch knew that for a fact a minute later, when they heard Sally's voice come through the hidden speakers.

'This is Captain Sara Wilcox and Lieutenant Cindy Makey of the Starship UFO. We demand your complete and unconditional surrender. You have two Earth minutes to comply. Failure to do so will result in your immediate and total destruction.'

Adam and Watch looked at each other in amazement.

Seven

Aboard Starship UFO – the name as well as their respective ranks had been Sally's idea – Cindy wondered if Sally had pushed it too far. Behind them, against the far wall, the two aliens huddled together as if afraid. Cindy worried they knew something their human enemies did not.

'Maybe we should negotiate a trade of prisoners,' Cindy said.

'This is interstellar war,' Sally said, her finger on the firing button. 'I don't negotiate.'

'But if you blow up their ship, you'll kill Adam and Watch,' Cindy pointed out.

Sally removed her finger from the firing button. They had figured out how to work the weapons – and navigate the vessel – on the journey out from the Sun. Of course the aliens had given them a few practical hints – when Sally had held the guns to their heads. Sally was showing the aliens no mercy. She yelled at them constantly, threatening to boot them out into deep space, where they would surely die. Cindy did not approve of the cruelty, even though the aliens would probably have killed them if given the chance.

'I know that,' Sally said. 'But I have to bluff with conviction. If I don't, Adam and Watch will never escape.'

'You don't know that for sure. A gentle approach might be better.'

Sally shook her head. 'Look who we're dealing with. These aliens land on our planet and immediately whip out their guns and kidnap our friends. We have to meet force with force. It's the only way.'

'Does it occur to you that the aliens in the other ship have a thousand times more experience at interstellar combat than you? What if they blow us out of the sky?'

Sally nodded. 'I thought of that. That's why I hit them hard first. I'm hoping we've already disabled their weapon systems.'

Cindy pointed to the large viewing screen above. 'You'd better pray as well as hope. They're coming around. And from the green glow around their sides, it looks like they're firing up their weapons.'

Sally spun on their captive aliens with a gun in hand. 'How do we raise our shields?' she demanded.

The aliens looked at each other with their big eyes. They shook their heads minutely, trembling as they did so, and hugged each other closer. They had earlier communicated with Sally and Cindy telepathically, but now they seemed too scared to send a clear thought.

'I think they're saying we don't have any shields,' Cindy said.

'We have to have shields!' Sally shouted. 'This is a spaceship. They always have shields in the movies.'

A hard blast, thick as a fist, struck their ship. Sally and Cindy went flying, and hit the floor. For a moment their lights failed and they were plunged into total darkness. It was terrifying; they could have been floating in empty space. Fortunately an emergency system came on, flooding the interior with a sober red light. Sally and Cindy crawled to their knees. Cindy felt a twinge in her right ankle. In all the excitement she had almost forgotten she was injured.

'They'll pay for that,' Sally said bitterly. She reached for the control panel, the firing button. 'We're taking no prisoners.'

Cindy stopped her. 'Wait a second. I hear something.'

'What?' Sally demanded.

'A telepathic message. Listen, here it comes again.'

Push the green button. Then the purple one.

'Did you hear that?' Cindy asked.

'Yeah, So what?' Sally pointed to the two quivering aliens, whose big black eyes looked ready to burst from their heads. 'They're just giving us instructions to blow ourselves up.'

Cindy got to her feet. 'They're more afraid of dying than us. The thought's not coming from them. It must be coming from the other ship.'

Sally was disgusted. 'Like we're going to listen to an order from them? Are you out of your mind? I say we return fire. If we lose Adam and Watch then at least they died in a good cause.' Once again she reached for the firing button. 'I'm locking on all our weapons. I'm going to maintain fire until one of us explodes.'

Cindy stopped her again. 'That's insane. We're not killing Adam and Watch.' She suddenly paused and went still. 'This thought feels different from the others. The person sending it seems to want to help us.'

Sally threw her arms in the air. 'The person sending this message is an alien! We can't trust it!'

Cindy spoke firmly. 'And we can't just keep blasting away. I say we give this message a chance. I know that sounds insane but somehow I trust it.'

Sally turned away in disgust. She glanced up at the ceiling. The other ship was coming round again. Sally could see them energizing their weapons.

'If you're going to respond to it, then you had better do so now,' Sally grumbled.

Cindy stepped to the control panel and pushed a green button, followed by a purple one. There was only one button of each colour on the panel. At first nothing happened. The other ship continued to bear down on them, its powerful weapon batteries glowing with a deadly green light. Then, behind her, Sally let out a gasp. Cindy whirled to see a little alien stand in the centre of their ship.

'Where did you come from?' Cindy exclaimed.

'*You just teleported me from the other ship. I am here to help you and your friends, Adam and Watch. May I use the control panel please?*'

'No!' Sally shouted, pointing her gun at the little alien. 'We're not turning over our ship to a runt like you.'

The alien stared at her calmly. '*I understand your lack of trust. I apologise for what my teachers have done so far to you and your friends. It is against our highest laws to infringe the free will of other intelligent creatures. I am here to help set the situation right. To do so, you must let me send a signal to the other ship. They will think I have taken control of this vessel and they won't fire upon it again. But if you don't let me take control, this ship, and you, will be destroyed in the next ten of your seconds.*'

'Let him do it!' Cindy cried.

'No!' Sally argued. 'It could be a trap!'

'We're already trapped!' Cindy shouted back. She glanced overhead. The other ship was still the same distance away. 'We have no choice, Sally. Can't you see that? Lower your gun.'

Sally hesitated, then angrily turned away. 'This is your call, Cindy. If you're wrong, I'm never going to let you live it down.'

'If I'm wrong, you and I won't be alive to live anything down.' Cindy nodded to the little alien, who was waiting patiently in the centre of the floor for their decision. 'Do what you have to do. Hurry!'

The alien stepped up to the control panel. He pressed a series of buttons. Outside, above them, the other ship suddenly veered off. Cindy let out a cry of relief, but Sally was far from happy. She pointed a finger at the little alien.

'I want our friends released right now,' she said. 'Then I want us taken back to Earth.'

The little alien stared at them as he spoke in their minds. *'That is not possible right now. I have no control over what my teachers on the other ship wish to do. And in a few of your minutes, they plan to jump through hyperspace and return to our home world. It is my suggestion that you allow me to follow them.'*

'What?' Sally cried, raising her weapon once more. 'Do you think that we're so primitive we'd fall for such a scam? If we go through hyperspace – whatever that is – we'll never get home. You turn this ship around right now. We're going back to Earth.'

'Sally, you have to control your temper,' Cindy said. 'It clouds your reasoning. We can't go home yet. We have to go where Adam and Watch go. And I trust this little guy.' She spoke directly to the alien. 'When we reach your home world, do you think we can get our friends released?'

The alien hesitated. *'It is possible. I have a plan. But it is a dangerous plan.'*

Sally shook her head. She continued to point her gun at the alien. 'Why should we trust you?' she demanded. 'Why should you betray your own kind to help us?'

'I do not betray my own kind by doing what is right. If my teachers are breaking our laws, then I am helping them by calling the criminal act to their attention. Also, I have studied your kind since I was very young. I have always admired you. I wish only to be of service.'

'A likely story,' Sally muttered. She glanced at Cindy. 'How can you trust a runt with such a fat head?'

Cindy reached over and patted the little alien on the head. The guy seemed to enjoy the attention. He moved a step closer to her, and touched her leg with his funny four-fingered hand.

'I don't know, I think he's kind of cute,' Cindy said. 'In a strange way, he reminds me of Adam.'

Sally snorted. 'If we get out of this, I'm going to tell Adam you said that.'

The alien looked at both of them. *'I should think Adam would be happy to be compared to me.'*

The situation was desperate. They were lost in space with aliens from another planet, and their friends were being held captive. But both Sally and Cindy suddenly burst out laughing. They could just imagine what Adam would say to that.

Eight

For Adam and Watch the jump through hyperspace proved unremarkable. They were racing into deep space – with the Sun now a bright star far behind them – when the aliens pushed a few buttons and there was a low hum. It lasted for only an instant. Adam felt as if everything went momentarily black. He felt a slight jerk; he might have twitched. Then he blinked and everything was exactly as it was before, only now the bright star was in front of them instead of behind.

'I thought the scenery would have changed more,' Adam muttered.

'So did I,' Watch said, puzzled.

'Are we sure we made the jump through hyperspace?'

'It seemed like it. Something happened.' Watch studied the stars through the wide ceiling. 'Maybe their solar system is not so far from our solar system, after all. Many of the constellations still look the same.'

'Are they the same?' Adam persisted.

'No. There are definite changes. For example, the Plough is bent out of shape. We must be seeing it from another angle. We have definitely travelled several light years in the last few seconds. But . . .' Watch trailed off.

'But what?'

Watch shook his head. 'I don't know what it is. Something is wrong here. I wish we still had our little friend to ask questions. I wonder where he went.'

'I get the impression he was teleported to the other ship. Notice how he stood real still in the exact centre of the floor. It was like he sent a mental signal to the girls to pick him up. Remember how he said his telepathic abilities had greater range than the adult aliens?'

'Do you think he's working for us?' Watch said.

'I hope so. Hey, that was pretty cool the way Sally just opened fire.'

'Yeah, she has guts. But she almost got us killed. I hope they follow us through hyperspace.'

'So do I,' Adam agreed. 'I think the little alien is our only ally in this part of the universe.'

Time crept slowly by. Adam and Watch began to feel hungry and thirsty. They complained to their captors but were completely ignored. Adam talked again about trying to jump the aliens, but he was now too tired to make the effort. Also, the more time that went by, the more he began to believe that the little alien was definitely in the other ship, and following them. Unfortunately they could see no sign of the other vessel. Perhaps that wasn't important. It was a big universe. The ship would have to be extremely close to be visible.

The sun up ahead continued to grow in brilliance. When it was about the same size as the Sun, seen from Earth, they saw a blue-white planet, with a silver moon circling round it. At first glance Adam thought he was seeing the Earth, but a closer look showed him that the continents and oceans were nothing like those of home. He felt a stab of despair. Even when everything had looked hopeless in the Haunted Cave, he had still been able to make constructive decisions. Here he was completely help-less. He had only a kid alien to rely on. Beside him, Watch pointed at the planet.

'See those glittering silver shapes orbiting it?' Watch said. 'I think each of them is either a space station or a space ship. This culture must be extremely advanced. Some of them look huge.'

'Maybe the aliens live in space,' Adam suggested. 'Maybe they polluted their planet so badly they can't live on the ground.'

'The way the human race is going, that might happen to us,' Watch said.

'If this alien race doesn't destroy us first,' Adam said. 'I've been thinking of the bigger picture. Our lives may not be all that is at stake here. What if they're preparing a huge invasion of our planet? What if they kidnapped us so they can torture us for what we know?'

'But we don't know anything,' Watch said.

'That's true – but they may not understand that. For all they know, kids from Spooksville may be the ruling class on planet Earth.'

'We certainly see more weird things than anybody else back home.' Watch continued to stare at the approaching planet and the silver chain of floating space ships and space stations. 'Your pollution theory might not be far-fetched. See that brown murky junk near that coast?'

'Yeah.'

'That looks like smog to me. Really bad smog. It's amazing, for all their advanced technology, that they haven't been able to clean it up.'

'It's easier to prevent a spill than to clean one up,' Adam said philosophically. 'But personally I don't care how messed up their world is. I just want to get home and have dinner.'

'Turkey and mashed potatoes would be nice right now,' Watch agreed.

'Is that what your aunt was cooking tonight?' Adam knew Watch did not live with either of his parents, or even with his little sister. But he had never asked his friend why the family was not together. The subject seemed too touchy. Watch lowered his head. 'My aunt never cooks,' he said softly. 'I have to prepare all my own food.'

Adam reached over and patted him on the back. 'You can come to my house any time for dinner. You're always welcome.'

Watch looked up and smiled faintly. 'You're only telling me that now your house is billions of miles away.'

Adam had to chuckle. 'Listen, when we were playing cards, how did you know Sally was bluffing? She acted exactly as if she had a strong hand.'

'The cards are marked.'

Adam was shocked. 'What? You mean you cheated?'

'Yes.'

'But that's terrible. Why play if you're going to cheat?'

'I can't see people's expressions as well as you guys can. So I mark the cards just to make it even.'

'Oh,' Adam said. 'When you explain it that way, I guess it isn't really cheating.'

'You can have your rocks back if you want.'

'That's all right. I'm not that into rocks.'

Watch pointed at one of the small viewing screens on the walls. 'See that huge cylindrical station? I think that's our destination. Look at the size of it! The station must be a mile long.'

Watch was right. The alien station was breathtaking in its size and obvious sophistication. It was like unto a miniature world in itself. And the most amazing thing was that there were thousands of others just like it in orbit.

The station rotated on its axis. But the flying saucer, as it approached, did not strive to match the station's speed, not exactly. It seemed as if they were going to enter the station from the top, in the centre, where there was no obvious movement at all. Suddenly a wide black door materialised in front of them. Adam was reminded of a hungry mouth, ready to swallow them. The saucer moved towards it. He shook his head sadly.

'Even if the little alien is helping us,' he said, 'I don't see how he can get us out of here.'

'It does look hopeless,' Watch agreed. 'But it usually does when you live in Spooksville.'

'We're a long way from Spooksville,' Adam grumbled.

The saucer flew into the station. For a moment all was dark. Then they came out into a massive chamber lit with soft yellow light. The wide space was a parking lot for saucers just like theirs. Literally hundreds floated nearby. Smoothly, their pilot manoeuvred past them. They seemed to be heading towards a dock of some kind. Adam knew that in a minute they would be leaving the ship. This deepened his depression. At least inside the spaceship, they had always had the chance of turning round and going home. Now that did not look on the cards.

There came a soft bump. The ship went completely still.

A door materialised to their left.

It led into a seemingly endless hallway.

The two aliens turned and drew their weapons.

The message was clear. Get up and get going.

Adam and Watch slowly stood and looked at each other.

'Are we having fun yet?' Adam asked.

'Sure,' Watch said. 'So much fun we might die laughing.'

The aliens escorted them from the flying saucer.

Nine

Sally and Cindy had indeed followed Adam and Watch through hyperspace. With the little alien's help, they were keeping far enough away to remain invisible. Yet Cindy believed the aliens on Adam's ship thought *her* ship's control had been returned to the aliens – the two cowards Sally had finally locked in the basement. Their pal had given that impression. He was trying to act like the hero in the fight between the aliens and the humans. Yet, although Cindy trusted him, she worried that Sally might be right. Maybe he was simply leading them into a trap.

But he seemed so sincere. As they ploughed towards his home world, he asked so many questions. They discovered he had been studying them since he was old enough to read.

'Why were you up in the hills by the water?'

'We were trying to cool off,' Cindy said. 'It's been hot

in our home town lately. We rode our bikes up to the reservoir. Did you see them?'

'No. Just before landing, my teachers made me go below.'

'They just didn't want you to see how cruel they are,' Sally muttered.

'That may be true, and if it is, I am disturbed. A report to our government must be made. The people must know what is happening.'

Sally snorted. 'On our world, if you make a report to the government, that's the last you hear about it. It's much better to get on TV.'

'I know your TV. I have studied it. You watch different shows. Some of them involve space travel, although your race is not yet advanced to travel much further than Earth orbit.'

'We've been to the Moon,' Cindy said. 'We might go to Mars soon.'

'If you know about our TV,' Sally said, 'you must have seen our programmes about you guys. We know about you aliens. We know you float down in the middle of the night and mutilate our cattle and steal our children. You can't underestimate us. If you try to invade, we won't be taken by surprise.'

The little alien paused and stared at her. 'I am not an alien. Do you not know that?'

Cindy spoke quickly. 'What Sally means is that you

appear alien to us. I'm sure on your home world you look just fine. There, *we* would be the aliens.'

'You would not be alien to us. That is not possible.'

'Then your people must be more accepting than ours,' Cindy said.

'They sure aren't any less violent,' Sally grumbled.

The alien lowered his head. *'My people are not perfect. We have our problems.'*

Time went by. Up ahead, the alien sun continued to grow in size as they flew towards the heart of the solar system. About three hours after they'd made the hyperjump, they caught sight of a blue-white world. Cindy and Sally were surprised to see that it had a moon circling it just like their own moon. For a moment the girls wondered if they hadn't simply flown in a huge circle. But it was not the case; they were far from home. Studying the planet, they didn't recognize a single one of the continents.

The little alien steered them towards a huge space station.

'Are you sure this is where Adam and Watch were taken?' Cindy asked as they neared the massive structure.

'Yes.'

'How do you know?' Sally demanded.

'I was informed by what you call radio.'

'Can the two aliens we have stowed in the basement communicate telepathically with your government and warn them that we have taken over this space ship?' Sally asked.

'I have erected a mental shield around this ship. I have set it so that only my thoughts are allowed in and out.'

'What do your people intend to do with Adam and Watch?' Cindy asked.

The huge space station was very near. They were coming in at the top. A black doorway opened before them.

'I do not know.'

'What reason did your teachers give you for going to our home?' Sally asked.

'They said we went there to observe. To learn.'

The ship slowed to a crawl. They began to enter the station.

'Well, I hoped they learned not to mess with us,' Sally replied. 'You said you had a plan to rescue our friends. What is it?'

'It is hard to explain.'

Sally fingered the weapon she kept tucked in her belt. 'You're going to have to do better than that. I have trusted you this far, but before I leave this ship I want to know what you have up your sleeve.'

The alien appeared puzzled. He checked his sleeve.

'I have nothing up it except my arm, Sally.'

Sally snorted. 'Just tell me how we're going to get our friends out of this metal cylinder.'

The alien thought for a moment.

'None of us is going to leave this ship. Not right now. I am going to try and start what you call a riot.'

'What?' Cindy gasped.

'I am going to broadcast the thought that your friends have been taken by force and are being held captive. I have explained that this act violates our most important laws. But I can only do this once I know where your friends are, and once I am hooked into what you would call a youth computer network. Except this network works with telepathy, not electric modems such as you have in your present day culture.'

Sally glanced at Cindy. 'Did you get all that?' Sally asked.

'I don't know.' Cindy spoke to the alien. 'Why do you first have to know where Adam and Watch are?'

'Young people play pranks in our culture as they do in your culture. I will have to prove that your friends are being held captive. The best way to do this is to direct as many individuals my age as possible to the place where Adam and Watch are.'

'What if they are in a restricted area?' Sally asked.

'Nowhere in our culture is supposed to be restricted.'

'Why do you have to be hooked up to a network?' Sally

demanded. 'Why can't you just broadcast the information with your fat head . . . I mean, just with your incredible telepathic abilities?'

'*It is easier on the network. It is set up so that interference is filtered out. I will be able to reach many more people this way.*'

'When you say a riot, do you mean that hordes of your kind will begin to loot and burn?' Sally asked.

The idea seemed to startle the alien. He took a moment to respond.

'*No. I mean that my people will gather and demand that Adam and Watch are released. It is the only way I can think of.*'

Sally glanced at Cindy and shook her head. 'I think our little friend underestimates what his government has going on the side.'

'What do you mean?' Cindy asked.

'Think about it. These ships obviously landed in Spooksville with the purpose of taking hostages. The aliens we hijacked weren't there to explore. They were there to grab some humans, pure and simple. That means they must have done it before, many times.'

'What are you saying?' Cindy asked.

'I am finally beginning to believe this runt is on our side. But I think he is naive. His government is no better than any government on Earth. It's up to all kinds of secret stuff that he knows nothing about. That's why they hid him out of the way when we were being kidnapped. Ten to one he's never going to be able to find out where Adam and Watch have been taken, especially if he stays inside this ship.' Sally paused. 'Did you hear that . . . What is your name anyway?'

'*Ekwee12.*'

'Do you mind if I call you Ek?' Sally said. 'No? Good. Did you hear what I just said?'

'*Yes.*'

'Well, what do you think?'

'*I hope you are wrong.*'

Sally had to laugh, but it was not a happy laugh. 'You can hope all you want. But I think we'll all be lucky to get out of this alive. One thing is for sure. As soon as we dock, there will be a group of guards waiting for us outside.'

'*No. I have already sent a message ahead that I have taken control of this ship. That is what I told my teachers on the other ship that I was going to do. There will be no guards waiting for us.*'

'Ek, I hate to tell you this,' Sally said. 'But you're about to get your first lesson in the real universe. This ship fired on the other ship. That is no small matter. Guards will be waiting for us and they will be armed. As soon as we dock, I want you to let them in and Cindy and I are going to hide behind the side of the wall. As soon as they're visible, we're going to stun them and then lock them in the basement with the other goons. In fact, would you set our guns to the right setting? I don't want to accidentally kill the guards. I would feel bad about it afterwards.'

Ek had to put a hand to his head. *'You will just shoot them if they come in?'*

'Yes,' Sally said. 'Listen, one of your guys already shot me tonight. And I woke up with a splitting headache. I have a right to a little retaliation.'

Ek gestured in front of them. *'We are about to dock. I should be able to tap into the network from here. I hope you are wrong about all this, Sally.'*

Ten

Adam and Watch were led to a sort of locker-room where they were told – telepathically – to undress and shower under a strange orange liquid. Actually, after all the bike riding and alien fighting, the shower was rather pleasant. The liquid was warm and smelt nice. Adam was happy to wash the dirt out of his hair.

But while they were in the shower, their clothes were taken. In their place was laid out two tan jump suits, similar to what the aliens wore, only larger. That was fine; neither of them was particularly attached to their clothes. They dressed quickly, enjoying the feel of the soft material against their skin. The only trouble was that Watch's glasses were missing. He stumbled about the room while Adam looked for them. The two observing aliens just stood there like statues, holding their ray-guns. Finally Adam got fed up.

'All right,' he said. 'What did you do with my friend's glasses? He needs them. He can't even walk down your long halls without them.'

At first the aliens acted like they didn't understand. They gestured with their guns for Adam and Watch to go through a door on the far side of the room. But Adam refused.

'We are not going anywhere until he gets his glasses back.' Adam pointed to his own eyes, then pointed at Watch's eyes. 'Understand? He uses those things to see.'

The aliens gestured again with their guns.

'No.' Adam crossed his arms over his chest. 'You're going to have to shoot us both. We are not leaving without those glasses.'

'Maybe you should tell them that they can shoot you if they want,' Watch said, bumping into a wall.

But the ultimatum worked. Finally they received a telepathic message.

'We did not know the glasses were so important.'

The glasses were returned and they were led from the locker-room area to a small cubicle that was equipped with an Earth-like toilet and two small beds set near the floor. The far wall of the room was made from what looked like clear glass or plastic; they could see through it into what appeared to be a courtyard. The moment they were inside the tiny room, the aliens turned and left, locking the door behind them. Adam pounded on it for several seconds, then gave up in frustration. There was not even a door knob he could try to break.

'This is a cage,' Adam muttered.

'It's one of many cages,' Watch said, standing near the far wall. 'Look out there.'

The courtyard was really a circular collection of twenty similar rooms. Each was equipped with a similar transparent wall, and held a different creature from a strange world. Some cells held two of the same species. In one glance, Adam and Watch were treated to an overview of many life forms from the local galaxy.

Closest to them was a creature that seemed to have six heads. Two metres tall, it was vaguely insectile; it walked about on six legs and had dozens of eyes on three of its heads, and tiny claws and mouths on the remaining three. It stared at them wickedly, with its many claws snapping repeatedly. Instinctively, Adam and Watch backed away from their transparent wall. The thing looked like it wanted to eat them.

In another cage was a blob-like being that seemed to flow from one corner of its container to another. There were fish creatures, birdmen, and one individual that looked like a cross between a robot and a dinosaur. They even saw what they thought was a hyeet – a Bigfoot. The hairy ape-like fellow waved to them. Adam waved back without enthusiasm.

'We're in a zoo,' he said miserably.

'I wonder,' Watch said, 'where all the tourists are?'

'Maybe it's night-time.'

'You wouldn't have night-time aboard a space station. People probably work in shifts. If this is a zoo, I would think it would be open all the time.'

'What are you saying?' Adam asked.

Watch scratched his head. The aliens had taken his four watches, and not returned them with his glasses. Adam knew how much his friend missed them. They were like part of his body, his persona even. Of course, if there was no night and day on a space station, then there were really no time zones either. Watch had an accepting nature. He had not complained of the theft.

'I think this is more of a laboratory,' Watch said finally. 'I think we're cut off from the public.'

Adam frowned. 'That sounds terrible. Do you think they will experiment on us?'

Watch nodded. 'It's a possibility. We have to mentally prepare ourselves to have our organs removed, maybe without anaesthesia.'

'If they remove many of our organs, we'll die.'

'It might be a blessing.'

Adam stepped back from the transparent wall and sat down on one of the beds. He was completely exhausted. The time he had spent unconscious from the ray-gun zap did not qualify as a refreshing nap. He was also deathly thirsty and hungry. He wondered what the meals would be like.

'You're depressing me,' Adam muttered.

'I'm sorry.' Watch sat on the bed across from him. 'Maybe it's not as hopeless as it appears. We've been in some nasty fixes before. We've always escaped. Why should this time be any different?'

'Because this time we're trapped in a cage billions of miles from Earth?'

Watch yawned and leaned back on the bed. 'Now you're depressing me.'

There was nothing else to say, for the time being.

They both laid down and rested. They may have even dozed.

Time went by. They were not sure how much.

Then they heard a soft knock at the door.

'Hey. Are you in there?'

Eleven

As Sally had predicted, when they docked there were four guards waiting for them. Sally got Ekwee12 to invite them in and Cindy and Sally stunned them from behind. They stored the guards in the basement with the other two aliens. To everyone's immense relief, no other guards rushed to the scene. Perhaps Ekwee12 was partially right. Their people were no experts when it came to security. There was time to work.

Unfortunately, Ekwee12 was making little progress with his plan. They had been in space dock an hour and he was still unable to locate Adam and Watch. He was searching through some kind of computer map, projected on to a three-dimensional computer screen located to the left side of the control panel. He said it was supposed to register all living creatures on the station, including ones like them.

'I do not understand why they do not show up.'

'It's like I told you,' Sally said, as she paced behind the Ekwee1 2. 'There are restricted areas aboard this station. You have to forget about trying to find them. Just broadcast on your telepathic network what has happened. Maybe one of the thousands of fat-heads . . . I mean, maybe one of your many network partners will have an idea where they can be found.'

'I don't know if that's a good idea,' Cindy said. 'The moment Ek makes such a broadcast, more guards will show up here.'

Sally was animated. 'I know that. I'm not stupid. But they're going to come here anyway. At least we will have got the message out. Once they arrest us, there will be no chance. We'll probably be put to immediate death.'

'Our culture does not have the death penalty.'

'You don't know what your culture does behind closed doors,' Sally snapped. Then she paused, thinking. 'How can we protect ourselves inside this ship? When they do come for us?'

'We can lock the door. But they will burn through it quickly, if they want to.'

'Can you fire this ship's weapons while we're in space dock?' Sally asked.

'That would not be a good idea. Many could be hurt.'

Sally rolled her eyes. 'Like I'm worried about a few

casualties. Listen, Ek, I am not a violent person by nature, but you guys started this, and I intend to finish it. When your authorities show up, we need something to fight them with until we can get Adam and Watch back. Better yet, we need something to *force* them to give us our friends back. Even if we just use it as a bluff.'

'What is a bluff?'

'It's what you do when you want to win at poker,' Sally said. She pointed to the floor beneath them. 'This ship accelerated to near light speed in two hours. It must have a powerful engine or warp drive on board. What's its source of energy?'

'*Our space drive is powered by the decay of an element called Zelithium 110. It cannot be found on your periodic table of elements because it does not exist naturally, except in the corona of extremely hot blue stars. As the element decays in a chamber of Hyperzoid Quartz, it radiates sub-atomic particles we call Bostonians. They are very powerful but unstable, unless carefully controlled.*'

Sally glanced at Cindy. 'I got less than half of that,' Cindy said.

'You say the Bostonians are unstable?' Sally said. 'I like things that way. They bring out my finer moments. Tell me, Ek, can this stuff be used to make a bomb?'

Ekwee12 looked as worried as an expressionless alien

could. 'Yes. *The Hyperzoid Quartz can be tampered with so that the decay of Bostonians builds towards a critical mass.*'

'What happens when a critical mass is reached?' Sally asked.

'*There is a huge explosion.*'

'Would the explosion be strong enough to destroy this space station?' Sally asked.

Ekwee12 hesitated. '*Yes. And many stations and vessels in the immediate vicinity.*'

'Can you control the decay of the Bostonians so that we don't accidentally blow ourselves up?' Sally asked.

'*Yes. But not well.*'

'Can you stop the chain reaction once it has begun?'

'*Yes. If I am lucky.*'

'If you start such a chain reaction, will the authorities outside know what you're up to?' Sally asked. 'Will they be able to monitor it?'

'*Yes.*'

'Will it scare them?'

The alien lowered his big head.

'*Yes. Very much. You could kill millions of my people.*'

Sally smiled at his sad thought. 'Ek, I don't want to kill anybody. I just want to scare your people into giving us back Adam and Watch. But when it is time to bargain, I have to give the impression that I'm a crazy chick from

Spooksville who would just as soon blow up this space station as go swimming in our reservoir at home.'

'What is Spooksville?'

'That's where we come from,' Sally explained. 'And you and your pals are only one of the reasons it has earned that name. You're not even the worst reason. Now broadcast your telepathic message about Adam and Watch and get your Boston bomb ready. Work as fast as you can. I'm still hoping to make it home in time for bed.'

Cindy shook her head doubtfully. 'You're playing with fire, Sally.'

'You don't understand me, Cindy.' Sally rubbed her hands together, excited. 'I'm playing to win.'

Twelve

Hearing the knock on the door, and the telepathic message, Adam and Watch jumped up from their beds and huddled by the door. They could hear nothing outside.

'Who do you think it is?' Adam asked.

'Either Ekwee12 or another alien,' Watch said.

'I know it's either Ekwee12 or another alien. Sally and Cindy haven't become telepathic in the last few hours. The question is, what should we do?'

'If it's someone come to rescue us,' Watch said, 'we'll never forgive ourselves if we don't answer.'

Adam put his mouth close to the door. 'Yeah, we're in here. But who are you?'

The telepathic response was immediate. *'Zhekee191.'*

Adam and Watch looked at each other. 'Their names are kind of corny,' Adam said.

'Imagine if there's hundreds of Zhekees,' Watch agreed.

Adam spoke to the door again. 'What do you want?' he asked.

'Are you two Adam and Watch? The two human beings?'

'Yes,' said Adam. 'How did you learn our names?'

None of the other aliens with the exception of Ekwee12, had asked them.

'Ekwee12 came on our youth network and explained that you two had been taken captive by our government, in violation of our laws. He wanted all of us to fan out and search for you. I know Ekwee12 personally. I am his friend and respect what he says. I know he would not joke about such a serious matter.'

'How were you able to get into this place?'

'My father works here. I have known for many years that we are not encouraged to visit here and it made me wonder if perhaps this was where you had been taken captive. I am pleased to find you so quickly. I have my father's pass key. It allows me to enter and exit this section.'

'Can you open this door?' Adam asked.

'Yes. I just have to push the button beside the door and it will open.'

Again Adam and Watch looked at each other. 'He might have said so at the beginning,' Adam said.

'Perhaps he's afraid how ugly we'll look,' Watch said.

'I know what you look like, of course. I will open the door.'

The door opened right then. Zhekee191 could have been Ekwee12's identical twin brother. He stared up at them with his big black almond-shaped eyes.

'*You are tall.*'

'We get taller, as time goes on,' Adam said. 'Where is Ekwee12?'

'*He did not say specifically but he must still be in the space dock.*'

'Do you know if he has our friends, Sally and Cindy, with him?' Watch asked.

'*No. He did not mention them in his message. Are they female humans?*'

'Yes.' Adam paused. 'How did you guess that?'

'*I have studied your culture. It is a required class in our culture.*'

'I didn't know we were so important,' Adam said. 'Are you guys planning to invade our planet?'

Zhekee191 seemed taken back.

'*We could not do that. It would not be possible.*'

'Then how or why do you know so much about us?' Watch asked.

'*Because you made us who we are. Of course.*'

'Of course,' Adam muttered. He had no idea what the alien was talking about, nor did he really care. He just wanted to get home. He was starving for a real Earth dinner. 'Can you take us to the space dock?' he asked.

'*That is what I wish to do. But we have to be careful. You are not easy to hide. I know a special way there that few take.*'

'Can you get us a weapon?' Watch asked.

'*What do you need a weapon for?*'

'Protection,' Adam said. 'We have already been shot by your people once today. We would not shoot anybody unless we were attacked. You have our word.'

'*I cannot get you a weapon. I do not even know where they are stored.*'

'Take us to the space dock then,' Adam said. 'And thanks in advance for all your help.'

Watch glanced back in the direction of the captured hyeet. 'I hate to leave that hairy guy. I feel like he's almost one of us.'

Adam nodded. 'Maybe we can rescue him later. But right now we have to take care of ourselves.'

They hurried out of the cell and raced down a long hallway. Right away Adam could see they were going a different direction from before. The hallways were similar to the others, but there were differences too. For example, after several hundred metres, they entered a glass hallway that looked out over a massive park area. The green area had to be miles across. It was crowded with thousands of aliens. Some seemed to be playing games, others were just relaxing by small lakes.

Yet there was no sun in the sky. There *was* no real sky, just a wide curving ceiling that glowed with gentle yellow light. Adam wondered if Watch might have been right. Maybe the aliens had polluted their planet so badly that they had to live in space, whether they wanted to or not.

Maybe that was why they kept coming to Earth.

To take it over.

Adam didn't care what Zhekee191 said. He was still worried about invasion.

Adam was glad no one looked up while they were in the glass hallway.

It would have been hard to outrun thousands.

But before they could reach the space dock, they did run into a guard. He appeared to be out looking for them. In his hand he carried a ray-gun and when he saw them he immediately aimed it at them. They received a strong and clear telepathic message.

'Stop where you are and put your hands over your head.'

Where they were, fortunately, was half a metre from a corner. Adam and Watch exchanged quick knowing glances. No way were they going back in that cage. They jumped for cover, behind the corner. There was a flash of green light – but it bounced harmlessly off the wall behind them.

Zhekee191 was taken by surprise. He continued to stand in the spot where the guard had spotted them. Watch moved to run away but Adam grabbed his arm and pulled him tight against the wall, right next to the corner.

'Let's take him,' Adam whispered.

The alien security guard had obviously not grown up on spy movies. The guy came running round the corner without any thought that they might be waiting for him. Adam simply stuck out his foot. The guy tripped; he went down hard. In fact, he seemed to knock himself out when his big fat head hit the floor. Adam reached down and grabbed his weapon, which had bounced free. Zhekee191 stared at them with a mixture of wonder and terror.

'You are an interesting species.'

'We have our good points,' Adam admitted. He showed Zhekee191 the weapon. 'How do I control the power on this thing?'

It was very simple. If he turned the little knob next to the handle clockwise, the power went up. There were ten settings. *One* stood for light stun. *Two* was hard stun. *Four* and up could kill, Zhekee191 warned. Adam left the weapon on *two*, where it had originally been set. But in his own mind he did not rule out the possibility of increasing the power. One way or another, he vowed, they were taking a space ship to Earth. Zhekee191 was more worried than ever.

'Please do not hurt anyone.'

'We only want to go home,' Adam said.

Zhekee191 led them on their way. Ten minutes later they reached the space dock. There was no transition. One second they were in a narrow hallway; the next they were in the gigantic space harbour. Adam and Watch were stunned to see a crowd of aliens gathered round one seemingly insignificant saucer. The ship floated at the end of a narrow dock. The aliens were bunched up on the dock like a can of sardines. They had several portable instruments with them. They seemed to be trying to measure what was going on inside the ship. The vessel looked exactly like the craft they had taken from Earth to the alien station. But Adam quickly realised that it was the one that held Sally and Cindy, not to mention Ekwee12.

Adam could dimly sense the buzzing thoughts.

The alien crowd was worried.

Adam planned to give them one more thing to worry about. He turned the power on his hand weapon up to *ten* and pointed it at the crowd. He had only been taught the rules of poker a few hours ago but he had learned them well.

'This gun is set to kill!' he shouted. 'Stand aside or I will fire!'

Thirteen

Ekwee12 had broadcast his telepathic network message to search for the humans some time ago. He had also started the Zelithium 110-Hyperzoid-Quartz-Bostonian chain reaction. The growing critical mass was definitely something the alien scientists could sense with their instruments – if the size of the crowd outside was any indication. Sally had already issued her demand for Adam and Watch to be released. She threatened to blow up the space station if they were not. But so far her friends had not been handed over. Sally believed that the chain reaction would have to get closer to the critical point before the aliens would do what she wanted.

But things were happening quickly.

At what Ekwee12 called Level 84 Bostonians, the reactor would blow.

They were now at Level 65.

Ekwee12 did not believe he could stop the reaction after Level 80.

'We're lucky they haven't tried to burn the door down,' Cindy muttered, watching the viewing ports along the wall.

Ekwee12 looked up from the control panel. *'They are afraid we will speed up the reaction if they try.'*

Sally continued to pace. The tension was growing unbearable.

'We're not leaving without them,' Sally muttered.

'I don't get you,' Cindy said. 'One minute you were ready to fly home without them. The next you're ready to sacrifice millions of lives to get them.'

'A girl has a right to change her mind,' Sally said.

'Are your people willing to sacrifice this station to prevent Adam and Watch from escaping?' Cindy asked Ekwee12, feeling desperate.

'I would have said no. My people cherish life. I do not understand why they are being so stubborn.' Ekwee12 glanced at his instruments. *'We have jumped to Level 72.'*

'So quickly?' Cindy asked, shocked.

'The reaction accelerates quickly as it reaches critical mass.'

'How much time do we have?' Sally asked.

'To stop the reaction, maybe three of your minutes. To the explosion, five minutes.'

'We have to back down,' Cindy said.

'We're not backing down!' Sally said. 'A bluff doesn't work unless you push it to the limit!'

'At the reservoir you were bluffing with rocks!' Cindy said. 'That wasn't gambling. *This* is gambling. You're risking our lives.'

'No guts, no glory,' Sally said. Yet she seemed uncertain. She paused in mid-stride, thoughtful. 'Ek, you have not recently checked your computer map of where everyone is supposed to be. Try locating Adam and Watch now.'

'What are you thinking?' Cindy asked.

'Maybe the aliens don't know where Adam and Watch are so they can't hand them over to us.'

'That's impossible,' Cindy said.

'Not if they've escaped,' Sally said.

Once again, Ekwee12 failed to locate Adam and Watch on his computer map. But it didn't matter, anyway. Glancing again out of the viewing ports, Cindy almost had a heart attack.

'There they are!' Cindy screamed. 'It's Adam and Watch!'

Sally pounded her fist in the air. 'I knew the bluff would work!'

'No!' Cindy said quickly. 'The aliens are not handing them over willingly. Adam has a gun. He's pointing it at the crowd. They must have broken free.'

'Just as I suspected,' Sally said. She turned to Ek. 'Open hailing frequencies.'

'*What?*'

'She wants to talk to the outside,' Cindy explained. 'Is there a way?'

'*Yes. Of course.*' Ekwee12 pushed a button. '*Speak and they will hear you.*'

'How close are we now?' Sally asked.

'*Level 75. We have less than two minutes to stop the chain reaction.*'

Sally cleared her throat and spoke loudly and formally. 'Adam, Watch – this is Captain Sara Wilcox of the Starship UFO. I am pleased to learn of your escape, and I approve of your resorting to blatant force to fight your way to freedom. But I feel an obligation to inform you that my starship is going to explode in two minutes and that everything for a radius of one thousand miles will be completely destroyed. Over?'

Outside, near the dock, Adam and Watch looked at each other. 'I think the power has gone to her brain,' Watch said.

'Is she bluffing?' Adam asked.

'I hope so,' Watch said. He gestured to the crowd of aliens that separated them from the ship. 'I think she's trying to scare these guys into letting all of us go.'

Zhekee191 shifted uneasily beside them.

'*She is scaring me. I would be happy to let you go.*'

Adam sighed, the gun still in his hand. 'I don't know what to do. I can't really fire this thing. I might hurt someone.'

'Somebody has to back down,' Watch said darkly. 'Or soon none of us will be feeling any pain.'

Inside the ship Ekwee12 informed Sally that they had jumped to Level 78. '*We have less than a minute.*'

'Why don't they let us go?' Sally demanded, getting exasperated. 'Can't they see that I'm serious? Do they want to die?'

'*I do not understand them. I do not understand why they kidnapped you in the first place.*'

'We must stop the chain reaction!' Cindy cried. 'The bluff has failed!'

'We can't stop!' Sally shouted back. 'If we do we'll never get out of here!'

'*We have jumped to Level 79.*'

'I would rather be alive here than dead!' Cindy yelled.

'Alive in a cage?' Sally demanded. 'That's no life!'

'I say we stop it!' Cindy shouted. 'And I have as much say as you! Ek, pull the plug!'

'*Which plug am I supposed to pull?*'

'Wait!' Sally cried.

'Wait for what?' Cindy screamed. 'Death?'

'Do it then!' Sally shouted bitterly, turning away. 'Surrender. That's all you're good for.'

Cindy bent over the control panel beside Ekwee12. 'Stop the reaction. Do it now.'

Ekwee12's four-fingered hands flew over the control panel. Then he sat perfectly still, waiting for some response to the chain reaction. He looked up at her with his big head. His whole body seemed to twitch.

'It is too late.'

'What?' Cindy cried.

'We have jumped to Level 81. Nothing can stop it from exploding.'

Cindy felt the life go out of her. She glanced over at Sally.

'Well, you got what you wanted,' Cindy said to her back. 'We're doomed.'

For a second, Sally froze, then she suddenly whirled on Ekwee12. 'Can we fly the ship out of space dock?' she asked. 'If we tell them we can't stop it, and they let us go, do we have time to get the ship clear of the station?'

Ekwee12 consulted his instruments.

'Yes. I can still manoeuvre the ship. If they let us go, we can move it out of the station before the explosion.'

'Talk to them,' Sally said. 'Send a strong thought,

whatever. Hurry!' Sally put a hand on Cindy's shoulder. 'You get off the ship. I'll ride out with Ek. I got him into this mess. If he has to die, I'll die with him.'

Cindy patted her hand. 'Sally, you amaze me. You're so brave.'

Ekwee12 jumped up quickly. *'They have opened the outside station doors for us. I have programmed the ship to fly into deep space. None of us has to stay here. None of us has to die.'*

'Actually,' Sally admitted, with a faint smile, 'I was hoping he was going to say that.'

The saucer door opened. They jumped out on to the dock. They were hardly clear of the ship when it took off at high speed behind them. They caught a flash of it going through the huge dark entrance – then it was gone. A minute passed while aliens and humans alike held their breath. Sally and Cindy waited for a huge shock wave, but none came. Then a wave of relief rippled through the gathering. Beside them, Ekwee12 calmly informed them that the ship had exploded safely out of the way.

'But we didn't feel anything!' Sally said. 'Was it a huge explosion.'

'Yes. But the ship is fast. It took place far from here, and there is no shock wave in space. You would not feel anything unless we were being destroyed.'

Sally nodded wearily. 'Well, it's done then. We're caught.'

The crowd parted so the four humans could at least be together. Adam surrendered his gun. There seemed no point in keeping it after a nuclear bomb had failed to move the aliens to release them. The guys patted the girls on their backs.

'Thank you for coming for us,' Adam said.

'That was an awesome bluff,' Watch agreed. 'I would have fallen for it.'

Sally shook her head. 'Not you. You're too cool a player.'

Watched glanced at Adam. 'I'm not saying anything,' Adam said.

There was nothing to say. Alien guards grabbed hold of their arms. The crude message was clear. They were going to be taken to the cages. Ekwee12 and Zhekee191 tried to protest, but they were pulled aside by the government authorities. Adam wondered what their punishment would be. He felt almost as bad for them as he did for himself and his friends. And they had come so close to escaping. It made the final defeat that much more bitter.

Yet all was not lost.

Suddenly, all around the circular space port, on maybe fifty different levels, young aliens poured into view. There were dozens at first, then hundreds. Within a couple of minutes, as Adam and his friends stood spellbound, the number swelled to at least two thousand. None of the aliens were over half a metre tall, but their combined telepathic message was very clear, and very powerful.

'LET THE HUMANS GO! THEY HAVE DONE US NO HARM!'

Ekwee12 broke free of the authorities and hurried to their side.

His thoughts were excited. *'These are my friends on the network. They are not going to let this injustice continue. They are demanding your release.'*

Adam laughed. 'Even us dull humans are able to pick up that kind of mental message. The question is, will your authorities do what your kids say?'

'I think they will have to. In our culture, kids are allowed to vote.'

'Cool,' Sally said. 'If that was true in our culture, I would be president.'

Another few minutes went by. The alien authorities huddled. The alien guards continued to hold on to the humans. But as time passed, more kids flooded the area. The huddled aliens seemed to grow even more uneasy. The young aliens' mental voice was like a huge washing wave of reason that could not be ignored. Finally a tall alien dressed in a gold suit took Ekwee12 aside. They conferred for a minute or two, then Ekwee12 ran to their side. He took Adam and Sally's hands and looked up at them with his big black eyes. Once again, he tried to smile. It was a good effort; this time there was real joy in the expression. *'They are letting you go. They have told me to take you home.'*

Fourteen

Far out in space, close to the hyperjump, Sally said that Cindy had said that Adam looked like Ekwee12. Adam was taken aback; he felt insulted.

'I don't believe Cindy said any such thing,' Adam replied.

'She did,' Sally said. 'Just ask her.'

Adam looked at Cindy. 'Well?'

Cindy hesitated. 'I said Ek *reminded* me of you. I didn't say you looked alike.'

'How do I remind you of an alien?' Adam wanted to know.

Ekwee12 spoke from his place at the control panel. '*We are both cute.*'

'That's it, exactly,' Cindy said with a smile.

Adam had to laugh. 'I suppose I've been called worse.'

'It makes me feel sick that he is flattered even by her insults,' Sally said to Watch.

'You're the captain,' Watch said. 'Why don't you have them both thrown overboard?'

'I've already gone to too much trouble to save them,' Sally muttered.

Ekwee12 turned and looked at them. *'We are almost up to the jump. I was wondering what precise time you would like to be returned?'*

That made them all sit up.

'Can this ship travel in time?' Watch said.

'Of course. You travelled in time on the journey here. Did you not know that?'

'How could we know?' Adam said. 'We thought this was just a regular space ship.'

'But you saw how much Earth had changed. You must have known we had jumped forward in time.'

They all stared at each other, shocked.

'Do you mean that you are from Earth?' Adam asked, barely able to get the words out. 'In the future?'

'Yes. I thought you knew.'

Sally was disgusted. 'But you're fat-headed . . . you're such an unusual alien shape. I don't understand.'

'I am not an alien. I told you.'

'But where have all the people on Earth gone?' Sally asked. 'Did you invade and wipe them all out?'

Ekwee12 shook his head. He must have picked up this

gesture from being with them. *'We are the people of Earth. We are what you will change into after another two hundred thousand years of evolution.'*

Sally was indignant. 'No way. My great-great-great-grandchildren are not going to look like you. I won't have it.'

'I think you need another two thousand "greats" in front of "grandchildren" to match the time frame he's talking about,' Watch said.

'If we do become you,' Adam said, 'why do you live in space?'

Ekwee12 lowered his head. *'You, we – we dirtied our planet. We cannot live there any more.'*

'But now that we know that,' Adam said hopefully, 'maybe we can work to stop people from polluting the Earth so much. I know I will try, as soon as I grow up and get out of Spooksville and get a real life.'

Ekwee12 raised his head. Once more he tried to smile. *'That could help us all.'*

'I don't know if I accept this,' Sally said. 'But for the sake of argument, say you *are* a more advanced form of us. Why would your people go into the past to steal us? For what purpose?'

'I meant to tell you this. When I conferred with our highest government official, he apologised and said that the government

had wanted a few kids from your generation to study to see how to liven up our culture. Lately we have become somewhat stagnant as a race.'

Sally laughed. 'He got more than he bargained for.'

'That is precisely what he conveyed to me. He thought we needed kids from an earlier, more calm generation. You guys were too explosive. But in either case, he promised that anyone else we took from the past would not be kidnapped. They could come with us only if they wanted to.'

'Can you see about getting that hyeet freed?' Watch said. 'He was in the cage across from us. He looked pretty miserable.'

'Now that we know the truth, the youth of our culture will demand that no intelligent creature is kept hostage. It should not have happened to begin with.'

'I agree with that,' Cindy said. 'This has been a long day.'

'That is what I am asking you. I can return you home at any time you wish. You have only to tell me when.'

'We should probably return just after we were kidnapped,' Adam suggested. 'After both ships left. I don't want to go running into myself.'

'I agree,' Watch said.

'Sounds good,' Sally said. 'That way we can make it home in time for dinner.'

But Cindy suddenly jumped up. 'We have to land before we left. We have to come in unobserved, and put down on the hill near the Haunted Cave.'

'Why?' they all asked.

Cindy was thoughtful. 'It's hard to explain. Just trust me on this one. Ek, do you have a ray-gun aboard this ship?'

'Yes. Why?'

'I will need to borrow it just after we land. Put us down just before the other two ships appeared. But like I said, don't let anyone – including ourselves – see us.'

'Cindy,' Adam warned, 'we don't want to tamper with time. Let our earlier versions have the adventure. It was fun, and it turned out all right in the end.'

But Cindy was adamant. 'No. This way is the only way. You'll see why when we get there.'

Cindy refused to change her mind, so they instructed Ekwee12 to do as she said. Ekwee12 adjusted the hyper-jump so that they burst through to their time a few hours early. In fact, he gave them enough leeway that they were able to swing by Jupiter, Saturn and Mars and have a look. Watch said the planets were much more impressive up close than in his telescope.

'I'm going to have to get one of these saucers,' he said with a sigh.

Finally, they landed on the hill near the Haunted Cave. Ekwee12 turned off the saucer's lights. They came down unobserved, then jumped out of the ship. It was still warm but it was good to be back, and feel normal earth beneath them. Even if they were in Spooksville once more, home was home.

Far below, they could see themselves sitting by the reservoir.

Cindy was still soaking her foot in the water.

'Oh,' said Cindy, wincing as she put her foot down. 'You guys will have to help me down the ravine. Ekwee12, I need that gun.'

'*Are you injured, Cindy?*'

'Yes. I sprained my ankle before you guys showed up.'

'*Why didn't you tell me? I have something that will fix that.*'

Ekwee12 disappeared inside. When he returned he carried a ray-gun and a small silver ball. Instructing Cindy to sit down, he placed the ball near her ankle. The ball began to glow a dull red colour. After a couple of minutes, Cindy let out a soft cry of delight. She flexed her foot and Ekwee12 withdrew the strange instrument.

'My ankle's all better! How did you do that, Ek?'

'*We know a lot more about human, and alien, bodies in our time.*'

'Great.' Cindy jumped up and grabbed the weapon. 'I have a job I have to take care of. The first setting is stun, right Ek?'

'That is correct.'

'Who are you going to stun?' Adam insisted.

'You'll see,' Cindy said. 'You guys can come with me if you're very quiet.'

Together, Ekwee12 included, they crept further down the hill, until they were almost able to hear the earlier version of themselves talking. No surprise, two alien ships suddenly appeared in the sky. They watched everything that had happened before, up until Watch was taken inside the first saucer. Then Cindy said they had to move closer.

'We shouldn't interfere,' Sally repeated.

'We won't,' Cindy promised. 'Everything will be just as it was.'

They crept cautiously around until they were at the lip of the ravine. Down below, the fighting started. Adam and Sally were stunned by the alien weapons. But back up on the hill, to everyone's surprise – except Cindy's – two aliens walked by just below them. To their even greater surprise they saw an earlier version of Cindy stand up on the opposite side of the ravine. She had a big rock in her hands.

Her intention was clear. She was going to brain one or

both of the aliens. They watched in amazement as she raised the rock above her head and threw it down. At that exact instant, *their* Cindy whipped out her gun and aimed and fired. There was a flash of green light. She stunned the aliens, and the two collapsed in a pile. The rock had missed by a mile. Cindy laughed quietly beside them in the dark as her earlier version peered confused over the edge of the ravine.

'I wondered why those guys just fell over on me,' she whispered.

Epilogue

It was time to say goodbye to Ekwee12. They hated to see him leave.

'Why don't you hang out with us for a while?' Adam asked. 'There's always a lot happening here. Things are never stagnant.'

'Yeah, you can learn a lot from us about how awesome kids are in this century,' Sally said.

'I would love to stay. But I have work to do at home cleaning up the confusion caused by your illegal capture. I have to return and make sure it never happens again.'

'But when you've finished your job, stop by some time,' Cindy pleaded. 'We like you. You're one of us.'

Ekwee12 held out his hands for each of them to touch. *'You will see me again, I promise.'*

They said their goodbyes. Cindy had a tear in her eye. Maybe they all did. But just as Ekwee12 was about to disappear inside his ship, Sally called one last question.

'Hey, Ek?' she said. 'Do you know why it is so hot here these days? We never have weather like this.'

'*A heavy inversion layer has settled over this portion of your coast. It will clear up in a couple of days and then you will have cooler temperatures.*'

'It's not a witch's curse, after all,' Adam teased her.

Sally nodded, insulted. 'I knew that.'

Spooksville 5

THE COLD PEOPLE

One

It was another Spooksville mystery.

The town was freezing, and it was still summer. The cold weather was as strange as the boiling temperatures had been a couple of weeks earlier when Adam and his friends had run into the aliens. None of them could understand what had brought on the chilly snap. That Monday morning, when they'd got up, every window in town was coated with a fine layer of white frost. Little did they know that, by the time the sun went down, there would be frost *inside* many of the people who lived in Spooksville.

Adam, Sally, Watch and Cindy started off the day by having their usual milk and doughnuts at the local bakery. Because of the cold, they each had a cup of coffee with their breakfast as well, just to warm their bones. To their surprise, Watch had a thermometer in one of the four watches he regularly wore. He studied it as they munched their food. He doubted the temperature would get above freezing all day.

'It's still in the low twenties,' he said. 'If we're going to be outside today, we better keep moving.'

They took Watch's suggestion to heart, and decided to spend the day hiking in the woods in the hills behind Spooksville. They pedalled their bikes most of the way there, hiding them in a cluster of trees when the road ran out. Adam had been up in the hills before, of course, when he had visited the Haunted Cave and the reservoir, but he had never been to the wooded area. He was amazed at the size and varieties of the trees.

'This wood looks like something out of *Hansel and Gretel*,' he said as they hiked along a narrow dirt path covered with pine needles. He wore a heavy jacket but unzipped it as he walked. The exercise was taking away some of the chill.

Sally snorted. 'Hansel and Gretel were lightweights. They only had one old witch to kill and it made them famous. We get worse than that every week and no one writes about us.'

'We need a press agent,' Watch agreed. 'Our life stories need to be on TV.'

'Personally I like being unknown,' Cindy said. 'I don't need all the money and fame.'

'Wait till you're a few years older,' Sally said. 'Money and fame will be what you crave the most.'

'I think all that stuff is superficial,' Cindy shrugged.

Sally sniggered. 'Spoken like a true liberal. In this world you've got to cash in when you can. For that reason I've started to keep a journal of my experiences. If I don't die in the next ten years, I figure I'll be able to auction the movie rights to my life.'

'Am I in your journal?' Adam asked.

Sally hesitated. 'You're mentioned in a small footnote.'

It was Cindy's turn to snigger. 'I bet the whole journal is about Adam.'

'That's not true,' Sally said quickly.

'Ha,' Cindy said. 'Prove it: let us read it.'

'You can read it,' Sally said. 'In exchange for a million bucks.'

As usual, Sally had the last word. They continued up the path without further conversation. Soon it began to narrow as the trees grew thicker. It could have been close to dark, the way the heavy branches hung over them. The shade was that deep. Yet Adam could still see his breath as he exhaled. Once again he wondered

3

at the strange weather and what could be causing it. He knew there must be a reason.

They were almost finished exploring and about to turn back when they spotted them: the Cold People. Adam saw them first, but initially he just thought they were huge blocks of ice jammed inbetween the trees. That in itself would have been strange enough but there was something even weirder: though there was frost in the surrounding branches, there was no actual snow. For that matter, the sun was still out; there were no clouds in the sky.

'Hey,' Adam said, pointing to a spot fifteen metres off the path. 'What's that?'

They all peered in the shadows.

'Looks like a glacier,' Sally said.

'The ice age would have to arrive for us to have a glacier here,' Cindy said.

'This town is not known for standard weather patterns,' Sally said. 'Two winters ago we had an iceberg float into our harbour. It stayed offshore for a couple of months. We had incredible snowball fights, until this polar bear came out of a hidden cave and ate Buddy Silverstone.'

Cindy snorted. 'I don't believe it.'

'There actually was an iceberg,' Watch said. 'But it

was an Eskimo who came out of the cave. And he just invited Buddy to dinner.'

'Yeah, but he didn't tell Buddy that he was the main course,' Sally said.

'Would you guys stop arguing and tell me what we're looking at,' Adam said.

Cindy squinted. 'Looks like big blocks of ice.'

'We know that,' Sally said impatiently. 'But what is the nature of these blocks of ice? Are they composed of frozen water? Are they from this planet? You have to ask yourself these questions.'

'Why don't we take a closer look?' Watch suggested.

It was a reasonable idea, although it was harder to get to the ice blocks than Adam had imagined. The trees were so compact in this part of the woods – Adam felt as if they would squeeze him to a pulp (no pun intended). But he told himself he was overreacting because of his first day in Spooksville when a tree had tried to eat him alive. And he had thought *that* was a strange day. Looking back, it had been pretty normal for this town.

There weren't just the two or three blocks of ice they had first seen from the path, but literally dozens of them. Some were lying down, others stood jammed between the tree trunks. They were almost all identical in size, two metres long by half a metre deep and half a metre wide. Adam and his friends knelt by the first one they came to. It lay flat on its back – and Watch tried to brush off the covering frost. But the block was only vaguely translucent; they could not see into the centre of it.

Yet there was something in there.

Something large and dark.

'These are like frozen coffins,' Sally said softly.

'Where did they come from?' Cindy whispered, fear in her voice. Up close, the ice blocks were sort of scary. Watch continued to brush the covering frost, hoping to come to more transparent ice.

'I don't think the ice-cream man put them here,' Sally said.

'This block is really cold,' Watch said, pausing to breathe on his unprotected hand. 'And I don't mean that it's ice cold.'

'What do you mean?' Cindy asked.

'Let me show you,' Watch said. He took off his watch that held the thermometer and laid it on top of the block. He left it there for perhaps ten seconds before he snapped it back up. He studied the reading. 'Ten degrees Fahrenheit,' he muttered.

'That's twelve degrees below freezing,' Sally whispered, amazed.

'That's a lot colder than the air temperature,' Adam said.

Watch nodded. 'Unless these blocks were just dropped here a few minutes ago – which I doubt – something inside them is generating incredible cold.' He tapped at the block with the knuckles on his right hand, then leaned over and sniffed it. 'I don't even think this is frozen water.'

'What is it then?' Cindy asked.

Watch frowned. 'It has a faint ammonia smell. But it's not ammonia.' He glanced at Adam. 'I would like to thaw one of these.'

'Do you think that's a good idea?' Adam asked.

'No,' Sally and Cindy said quickly together. They glanced at each other in surprise. It was seldom they agreed upon anything. Sally continued, 'There may be something inside we don't want to thaw.'

'Like what?' Adam asked.

Sally shook her head darkly. 'You know this town. We could have anything from a bloodthirsty vampire to a blob from Planet Zeon inside here. I have a personal rule against fooling with strange artefacts that might end up eating me.'

'That rule must make your journal pretty boring,' Cindy remarked.

'There is a coincidence here that we're forgetting,' Adam said. 'It is freezing today and it's still summer. These blocks are colder than freezing. Is it possible there is a connection between the two?'

Watch nodded. 'You make a good point. But I can say for a fact that these blocks alone are not cooling off this entire area.'

'I'm not saying that,' Adam replied. 'I mean that these blocks may have arrived here today because it is cold.'

'You mean whoever put them here might be behind the cold?' Cindy asked.

'Exactly,' Adam said.

'I think we have to take the risk,' Watch said. 'We have to thaw one. It's possible that there's nothing inside.'

'I have my Bic lighter,' Sally said reluctantly. 'We could gather some dry sticks and build a fire beside it.'

'But the fire might hurt whatever is inside the block,' Cindy said.

'Personally I'm not worried about that,' Sally said.

'If we're careful with the flames,' Watch said, 'I'm sure we can avoid damaging the contents of the block.'

Adam nodded. 'I do think we have to have a look at what's inside. I know I won't be able to sleep

8

wondering about it. As long as we all know that once we have thawed whatever this is, we probably won't be able to freeze it again.'

Sally agreed. 'This is like opening Pandora's Box. There'll be no turning back.'

Two

They did not have to go far to gather the necessary sticks and twigs to build a fire. Even though it was a cold day, the area was still dry. Soon they had a respectable pile of wood beside the ice block. Sally took out her lighter.

'Why do you carry a lighter anyway?' Cindy asked. 'Are you thinking of taking up smoking when you're sixteen?'

Sally made a face. 'You will recall how many times we wished we had a lighter in the last four weeks. This place is unpredictable. If I wasn't such a pacifist, I would carry a gun in my other pocket.'

Cindy smiled. 'You're as much a pacifist as a hungry mountain lion.'

'What does *pacifist* mean?' Adam asked Watch.

'Sally when she's totally unconscious,' Watch

11

replied. 'Light the pile, Sally, and move back. Adam, Cindy – you also get back. I'll take care of the flames.'

Sally flicked her Bic. In the deep shadows of the surrounding trees, the orange flame glowed bright. Sally moved it towards the pile of sticks and twigs.

'Are you worried something might jump out and grab us?' Sally asked.

'There's no reason to risk all of us,' Watch said.

The flame immediately caught. In seconds they had a crackling fire. The dark smoke gathered beneath the frost-covered branches. The white flakes thawed, and drops of water fell around them. But the block of ice thawed much more slowly. Taking Watch's advice, Adam had moved back a metre or so. But he could see that the block was hardly reacting to the fire. He pointed that fact out to the others.

'It confirms what I suspected,' Watch said. 'This block cannot be frozen water. It must be some other chemical substance with a much lower freezing point. Hand me a couple of those logs behind you, Cindy. We need a bigger fire if we're going to get anywhere with this thing today.'

So Watch threw a couple of *real* logs on the fire. This wood took a few minutes to catch, but soon enough they had a roaring fire going. The smoke continued to gather beneath the branches, creating a black cloud that caused them all to start coughing. But now, finally, the block began to melt.

The liquid, as it dripped off, was a dull blue.

It fell in a puddle around Watch as he sat beside the block. Steam rose from it. Blue steam. It mingled with the black smoke, creating a ghastly colour.

The block started to grow clearer.

There was definitely something inside.

Something human-shaped.

It could have been a man. A very cold man.

'Watch,' Adam said softly. 'I think maybe you should sit back with us.'

'Yeah,' Sally whispered. 'I don't like what I'm seeing.'

Watch shook his head. 'I have to control the fire. I can't burn him.'

'Is it a *him?*' Cindy gasped.

'I think so,' Watch said. 'And if it is a person, he's got to be dead. He can't hurt us.'

'I wouldn't necessarily make that statement about all dead people in Spooksville,' Sally said.

The ice – or whatever it was – continued to thaw. A hand became visible, then an arm. The latter plopped out as the heat of the flames dug deeper into the block.

The exposed flesh glistened in the light of the flames. Soon they were staring at the exposed side of the man. He was not naked but wore what looked like a blue jump suit. Yet his skin was very pale. Of course, he was a corpse – he was supposed to be pale.

'Is he alive?' Sally asked.

'He was frozen,' Cindy said. 'He can't be alive.' She paused. 'Is he alive?'

Watch carefully poked his skin. 'I don't think so. He's not moving or breathing and he's too cold.'

'I don't think you should touch him,' Adam said. 'He might not like that.'

'Dead people don't like or dislike anything,' Cindy said.

'I know a few dead people who have very specific tastes,' Sally said. 'But I agree with Adam. Don't touch him. You might catch some disease.'

Watch ignored them. He picked up the man's hand and studied the palm. 'Incredible,' he whispered. 'He has no lines on his hands. No prints on his fingers.'

'But aren't fingerprints created in the womb?' Adam said.

'Yes,' Watch said. 'I don't think this guy was ever in one.'

'What are you saying?' Cindy demanded.

'He's saying this guy was never born,' Sally said, her tone anxious. 'And if that's the case, he might never have really died. Watch, get away from him *now*. You're making me nervous.'

It was a pity Watch did not immediately take Sally's advice. If he had, maybe he would have got away. Maybe they all would have. But Watch did not listen and he did not get away.

Watch was poking at the man's palm when the hand came alive.

The fingers moved. They bent into a claw shape.

Watch dropped the hand and sat back.

But the cold man's arm was long.

It reached out and grabbed Watch by the foot.

'It's got me!' Watch cried as he tried to shake loose. 'Help!'

They jumped to his side, crowding round the fire. Adam went down on his knees beside Watch's foot and tried to pull the fingers apart with all his strength. But they were like marble; they did not budge. The hand began to pull Watch towards the block of ice. Sally grabbed a stick and began to pound the arm. Cindy kicked at it with her feet. Still, the cold arm continued to drag Watch towards the block.

15

'Grab a stick out of the fire!' Watch shouted. 'Press it to its skin!'

Unfortunately they all turned to follow Watch's advice at once. It was a shame because at that exact moment, when their backs were to the block of ice, it exploded. The shards of ice fell on them, debris of the blast. For a moment they didn't even know what was happening.

Then they saw that the cold man had broken free.

He was standing upright. Holding on to Watch.

The cold man opened his eyes and stared at them.

His eyes were blue, completely blue. There were no pupils, no eyelashes. The eyes shone with a strange light that sent shivers down their backs. Now the man had his arm round Watch's neck. He clearly had no intention of letting him go.

'Use the fire,' Watch called, shivering uncontrollably. 'Try to force him to release me.'

'Maybe we could ask him to let you go,' Cindy cried. 'Hey, you big popsicle, let our friend go!'

In response the man stared at Cindy and the strange blue light from his eyes seemed to envelop her. Cindy backed away and screamed.

'He's freezing me!' she said.

Adam had seen enough. He already had a

smouldering stick in his hand. He rushed towards the creature, waving his torch in the air. The man turned away from Cindy and retreated, but he continued to hold on to Watch.

'Let him go or you burn!' Adam shouted. 'Sally! Go round his back.'

'Gotcha,' Sally said, a torch in her hand as well. She split from Adam's side and tried to get behind the creature. But the trees were too thick; she could only come in at his right side. The cold man's head darted from side to side. Clearly it did not like the fire, yet it was willing to risk holding on to Watch. Every time Adam tried to make a stab at the thing with his torch, it blocked his way using Watch as a shield.

'What should I do?' Adam called to Watch.

'It's so cold,' Watch moaned, his lips actually turning white, as if he were freezing to death where he stood. 'Try threatening one of his partners.'

'I'm on to that,' Cindy said grabbing a particularly big torch and taking it over to another block of ice. She held it close to the ice and called back at the cold man. 'Let him go or I fry him!'

'It might be a her,' Sally said.

Once more the cold man concentrated his weird glowing eyes on Cindy. A blue light leapt towards her like an icy sword. Before Cindy could even raise her torch to ward off the freezing beam, her arm went numb. She tried to speak but only choked sounds came out. Adam thought she might freeze or suffocate in the next minute. Not having a chance to think of another plan, he threw his torch in the air, over the cold man's head. It landed at his back and once more the cold man was forced to withdraw his icy gaze. But this time he did not give them a chance to regroup.

Tightening his grip on Watch, he turned and leapt into the trees. He was very quick. He was out of sight before they could react.

In the shadows of the forest, they heard Watch scream.

Then there was nothing but horrible silence.

The cold man had taken their friend.

Three

They put out the fire. The flames appeared to be their only defence against the cold man, but they were afraid the heat might awaken another of the creatures. Yet they kept their torches, and they went after Watch.

It was hopeless from the start. The wood was so dense that it took them half an hour to get a hundred metres. Plus, clearly the cold man could move many times faster than them. They went after their friend with heavy hearts. They knew they were not going to find him, not without help. As they paused to catch their breath beside a gurgling stream, Adam stared at their dying torches and shook his head.

'We have to go back to the path,' he said reluctantly. 'We can't face the cold man without fire, and these sticks will burn out in a few minutes.'

'But we can't leave Watch,' Cindy cried. 'Remember

when we were trapped in the cave? He did everything he could to rescue us. We have to do the same.'

'I agree with Adam,' Sally said sadly. 'We can't help him this way. We need reinforcements, better weapons. We have to get back to town and warn everybody what's happening.'

'No one will believe us,' Cindy said. 'If you told me this story, I wouldn't believe it.'

'But you don't believe anything I say,' Sally replied.

'We'll have to deal with that problem when we come to it,' Adam said.

'But what are we going to tell people?' Cindy persisted. 'We don't even know what these creatures are. We have no idea where they came from.'

Sally was curious. 'What was it like when he stared at you?'

Cindy lowered her head and shivered. 'It was as if the blood in my veins was turning to ice – literally. And there was something else – it was like the cold man hated me for being warm. I felt his hate, his envy.' A tear slipped down her cheek. 'I hope Watch is all right.' She raised her head and stared at Adam. 'You do think he's still alive, don't you?'

Adam wanted to say something encouraging, but he felt Cindy would see through his lie. He thought of how strong the cold man was, how quick he moved. How powerful his strange eyes were. In reality Adam did not have much hope for his friend.

'I just don't know,' Adam said quietly.

Their bikes were where they had left them. The road back to town was mostly downhill. They'd never pedalled so fast in all their lives. The cold wind blew in their faces. Their cheeks burned and froze at the same time. Adam wanted to ride straight to the police station but Sally wanted to find Bum first.

'Bum knows much more than the police,' she said.

'I thought you didn't trust Bum?' Adam asked.

'I trust no one,' Sally said. 'But Bum likes Watch. He'll do anything to rescue him.'

They found Bum down at the beach, feeding the pigeons. He seemed happy to see them, at first, but when they related what had happened, he sat down with a weary thud. His glum expression worried them. They could have come to tell him about the breakout of a nuclear war and he would have laughed it off. He was that easy going. But there was something in their story that pushed a deep button in him.

'It's the Cryo creatures,' Bum muttered.

'What are they?' Adam demanded.

'Cryo means cold,' Sally offered.

'We know that,' Cindy said impatiently. 'But what are these creatures?'

Bum sighed. 'To put it bluntly, they're bad news. I haven't heard of them in a long time. In fact, they haven't ever appeared during my life.' He paused and shook his head. 'You say they got Watch?'

'Yeah, one of them has,' Adam said. 'What will it do to him?'

'Make him cold,' Bum said softly.

'That's all?' Cindy asked hopefully. 'It won't kill him?'

Bum put his hand to his head. 'You misunderstand me. It would be better if it killed him. When I say it will make him cold, I mean it will turn him into one of the Cryo creatures.'

Sally's face fell. 'You mean it will turn Watch into a monster?'

Bum spoke darkly. 'By now it has already changed him. There is no Watch any more. If you see him, he will try to change you.'

Adam felt his heart breaking. 'But can Watch be changed back into a human?'

Bum rubbed his head. He appeared to be thinking hard what to do.

'I don't know,' he said. 'I don't think so. These Cryo creatures – they are very ancient, and their power is very great. We may all be doomed.' He nodded to the ground beside the ocean wall where he sat. 'Make yourselves comfortable. I have a story to tell you. It isn't a pleasant story, but you have to hear it if you're to know what you're dealing with.'

Adam sat, although he felt rushed. 'Can you give us the short version? We have to try to help Watch, no matter what you say.'

'You can help him most by listening for a few minutes,' Bum said. 'But what I have to say – you don't have to believe any of it if you don't want. I don't care. You can just see the story as a myth. But I can tell you that I believe it.'

Bum paused to clear his throat. As he told his story, he stared out at the ocean.

'A long time ago the world was not as it is now. You have probably heard of the lost continent of Atlantis, which was supposed to be located in the Atlantic ocean. Atlantis really did exist, and during the same time period there was another land that has since vanished. This one was in the Pacific Ocean and it was called Lemuria, or Mu for short. It was at least twice the size of Atlantis. You may be surprised to know that parts of

23

the West Coast were once part of Mu. Spooksville, for example, used to be an eastern city of Mu. I have often thought that one of the reasons Spooksville is such an unusual place is because it really belongs to another era. But that is a story for another time.

'Atlantis and Mu existed for tens of thousands of years, but the two lands were not always on the best terms. Actually, they spent a lot of time fighting, but they had so much history together, they were also good friends for centuries at a time. However, they could never stay friends, and the main reason was because they were never left alone. You see, in those days the technology was far more advanced than it is today. They had machines that could beam you from one side of the planet to the other. Ships that could travel to other galaxies.

'I know in school your history teachers never talk about these things. Few people in the world realise how old civilisation really is. How old mankind is. You see, we did not originate on Earth, but came from a star cluster called the Pleiades, or the Seven Sisters as it is better known. You can see it in the winter sky if you look up on a dark night. The cluster is hundreds of light years from Earth. Our most ancient ancestors came from worlds circling those blue stars. But the people of the Pleiades – their ancestors came from somewhere else. From a world that was long ago destroyed. It's true – I think it's true. No one can really say where it all started.

'People from the Pleiades and other worlds often visited Earth. Their spaceships landed in Atlantis and Mu. The trouble was, not the same star people visited Mu as visited Atlantis. There are many Pleiades worlds, at least dozens. They don't all get along either, or at least they didn't back then. I don't know how they're doing these days. The witch – Ann Templeton – might know. Some say Madeline Templeton, Ann's great-great-great-great-grandmother, was really from one of those worlds. But that, too, is another story.

'So we had these two large lands, Mu and Atlantis, and they were being told what to do by different races from the stars. And these different star people didn't like each other. Towards the end of Atlantis and Mu, the star people were at war, and they wanted the people of Earth to join their war – they saw the Earth as just another battlefield. It was a mess. The scientists from one planet were telling the people of Atlantis how to make a bomb to blow up Mu. While other star scientists were telling the people of Mu how to blow up Atlantis.'

Adam interrupted. 'Why didn't the people of Earth just tell these guys to get in their spaceships, fly away and leave them alone?'

Bum nodded. 'That's a good question. The reason the Earth people didn't kick them out is because the star people knew more than they did. True, the Earth had originally been settled by the star people, but that had been millions of years before all this went on. By the time the star people returned and brought their troubles, people on Earth were way behind them. The star people had machines and devices that would have taken Earth people thousands of years to discover. I guess you could say the star people bribed the Earth people. 'If you do this for us,' they would say to our leaders, 'we will give you this secret.'

'But what does all this have to do with the Cryo creatures?' Sally asked.

'I am just getting to that part. I had to explain these other things first.' Again Bum paused to clear his throat before continuing. He sounded hoarse. Adam wondered if he had a cold. Adam imagined sleeping outside all the time was not easy.

'I have to make it clear that not all the star people were evil,' Bum went on. 'You know in any war there are good guys and bad guys. But I don't think in this war all the good guys were on one side. I think it was mixed. Many of the star people who helped Atlantis really thought they were doing the right thing. I'm sure many of the star people who helped Mu thought they were the good guys. But I do know it was the star scientists on the Mu side that made the Mu leaders a really evil offer. An offer so tempting that the Mu leaders could not resist.'

'If it was an evil offer,' Cindy asked, 'why was it so tempting?'

'Evil is always more tempting than good,' Sally said. 'That's life. All the fun things get you into trouble.'

Bum paused and smiled, although he remained serious. 'Sally might be right, I'm not sure. But I do know that one secret group from the Pleiades told the leaders of Mu that if they would completely wipe out Atlantis, they would be given a chance to live for tens of thousands of years.'

Adam was impressed. 'Did the star people live that long?'

Bum scratched his head. 'They lived a very long time, much longer than Earth people. The leaders of Mu could see that. Each time the star people visited – every few years – they would have hardly aged at all, while the Earth leaders would be getting old and

27

wrinkled. These evil star people convinced the leaders that they didn't have to die. And that was a lie. Even the star people died, eventually. It was just another bribe, a false bribe. Yet there was truth in it as well. Let me explain.

'If you cool something down, it lasts longer. If you freeze it, and keep it frozen, it lasts practically for ever. You can do this with a hamburger: keep it in your freezer and you can eat it a year later. The meat won't have spoiled. But the second you take the meat out of the freezer and begin to thaw it out, it begins to grow old. Leave it out for a few days and it will rot. Do you get my point?'

'Yes,' Adam said. 'But you can't freeze people to make them live for ever. If you freeze someone they can't move. They die.'

'That is true with the technology we have now,' Bum said. 'But you mustn't forget these visitors from the stars knew things we can't imagine. They told the leaders of Mu that, in exchange for wiping out Atlantis, they would show them how to transform the cells of their bodies so that they lived on a freezing substance called cryo, rather than on warm blood. Don't ask me what this cryo was made of – I don't know. But somehow it allowed a person to be colder than ice and yet still be able to walk around and do things like a living person.'

'Did any of the star people have cryo in their veins?' Sally asked.

'That is another good question,' Bum said. 'The answer, as far as I know, is no. None of the star scientists visiting the Earth were Cryo creatures. That should have warned the leaders of Mu that something was fishy. But I think these leaders were all selfish people, cowards, afraid of death. They took the bribe. They thought they would wipe out Atlantis and in exchange they would be made immortal.

'It is not an easy thing to destroy a continent. Even with nuclear bombs, you can't just make a whole land mass vanish. What the leaders of Mu decided to do was get a little help from the asteroid belt. You know, it's out there between Mars and Jupiter – a bunch of huge rocks floating round the sun. These guys – they may have been evil but they were pretty clever. They hooked rockets and space drives on to a particular asteroid and began to steer it towards Earth. They adjusted the speed and direction precisely. Just as Atlantis was coming round – as the Earth rotated – the asteroid was right there. A gigantic rock flying right towards them.

'Of course the people of Atlantis saw it coming. It

was hard to miss – it darkened the entire sky. In the last hours, they knew they were about to be wiped out and they knew the leaders of Mu were behind it all. But what they didn't know was that those leaders weren't even human any more.

'But I have to back up for a moment. Once the Mu leaders had directed the asteroid towards Atlantis, they had fulfilled their part of the bargain. Never mind that the asteroid took a few weeks to reach the Earth. Even before it became visible in the sky, the evil star people drained the blood of each of the leaders of Mu and replaced it with cryo. Then the star people quickly left. Maybe they left laughing.'

'Why?' Adam interrupted, fascinated by the tale, even though he was not sure if he believed it. Bum was right – he had never seen any of these things in his history books at school. Then again, he had yet to go to school in Spooksville. Maybe they had a whole class devoted to pre-history history.

Bum replied to his question seriously. 'Because the cryo made the leaders stop aging, but it did other things to them as well, some of which were not so pleasant. The leaders became super strong and super fast. They also gained a strange power of vision. They could not only see far away, they could freeze people by their mere glance. In fact, they could make others like themselves, if they wished.

'The problem was they were not really alive. They did not *feel* alive. They just felt cold all the time, and they hated the cold. They were like the walking dead. They envied normal people. True, they would not die for a very long time, but they could not enjoy anything. They saw this right away, even before the asteroid reached the Earth. They realised they had been tricked by the evil star people.

'But back to the asteroid. Like I said, it was headed straight towards Atlantis and the people there knew who had aimed it at them. But despite all their technology, they could not stop it. An asteroid can be pretty big. This one was over thirty kilometres in diameter and it was travelling at hundreds of kilometres a minute. Sure, the people of Atlantis shot nuclear missiles at it, but it just kept coming. They were in a real bind.

'They didn't want to lie down and die, at least not without getting revenge. Just as the asteroid began to near the atmosphere, they fired off every weapon they had at Mu, and they had a lot of weapons. From coast to coast, Mu burned. Then, when the asteroid did strike, Atlantis was crushed beneath the Atlantic ocean.

Worse, it was forced beneath the Earth's crust. That is why there is almost no sign of it these days. The geological plates of the Earth shifted under the blow of the asteroid. Mu, which was already burning, also slid under the Pacific ocean. Both great lands were destroyed together. Both great civilisations were wiped out, and people don't even remember them today.' Bum paused. 'I think it's a sad story.'

'But what about the Cryo creatures?' Sally insisted. 'They're our problem right now.'

'Yeah,' Adam said, although he had enjoyed the story. 'Didn't they all die when Mu was destroyed?'

'No,' Bum said. 'Some of them escaped. From what I understand, several figured out ahead that Atlantis would attack before the asteroid hit. They left Mu and travelled to the north pole where they dug themselves into a valley of ice. They survived the fire from the bombs and the asteroid.' Bum stopped. 'But now they've come back.'

'Why?' Adam asked. 'Why here? Why today?'

Bum was thoughtful. 'They may have come here because Spooksville is one of the few surviving pieces of Mu. But why they have come today, I don't know. From what you described, someone must have brought them here – since they were frozen solid. But who that someone was – your guess is as good as mine.'

'All this is very interesting,' Sally said. 'But how do we stop them, other than blowing up all of Spooksville?'

Bum spoke seriously. 'That might be the only way to stop them. This city is not the only place in danger. From what I know of their history, the Cold People – that's their more common name – could sweep over the entire world. It may have been a good thing Mu was destroyed when it was. Before the asteroid hit, the Cold People who remained in Mu were already altering their own people. They're like vampires, except they like frost instead of blood.'

'Look,' Adam said, getting impatient. 'We can't blow up Spooksville. We don't have nuclear bombs. You have to give us a second option.'

'You mentioned how the creature fled from the fire,' Bum said. 'That's the key. We have an army surplus store just outside of town that sells all kinds of exotic war equipment. They have a few flame throwers. You might want to buy them.'

'They're not going to sell flame throwers to a bunch of kids,' Cindy protested.

'They might,' Sally said. 'I know the owner of the store, Mr Patton. He copied his name from the famous general. He believes every man and woman should walk round armed at all times. He'll sell you a tank if you have the money.'

Bum nodded. 'He might even give you the equipment on credit, if he's convinced the city's really in danger.'

'Aren't you going to come with us?' Sally asked. 'We need your help if we're to fight these things.'

Bum scratched his unshaven chin and thought a minute. 'I would rather leave town and try to forget that any of this is happening.'

'Coward,' Cindy muttered under her breath.

Bum half smiled. 'I said I would rather leave. I didn't say that I would. Sure, I'll help you fight them. God knows if we don't stop them here, we'll never stop them.' Bum stood. 'Come, let's get to the surplus store.'

Cindy appeared to have reservations about their plan.

'Why don't we go to the police?' she asked. 'That's what they're there for – to help in times of emergency.'

Sally snorted. 'That may be true in other cities, but in Spooksville the police are afraid to answer a call to get a cat out of a tree. They've seen too many of their buddies go out on calls and never return.'

Cindy was doubtful. 'I think we have to warn them at least. Adam, would you come with me? We can catch up with Sally and Bum in an hour or so.'

'An hour is a long time when you're dealing with creatures that can multiply,' Sally warned. 'But of course Adam will go with his dear Cindy just because she asked. He does whatever she asks because he loves her, and she acts like she loves him. It doesn't matter that the safety of the entire world is at stake. Isn't that true, Adam?'

'Well,' Adam said, caught off guard. 'I think we should let the police know.'

Sally and Bum exchanged knowing glances.

'We'll pick out the flame throwers,' Bum said.

'We'll have them gift-wrapped before these guys show up,' Sally agreed.

Four

The Chief of Police of Springville – Spooksville's proper name – was alone in the station when they arrived. There was not even a secretary around, never mind more officers. There was just the Chief sitting behind his big oak desk, reading a comic book and eating a box of chocolates. From his large belly, it appeared he often ate chocolates.

They knocked before entering but nevertheless startled him. He glanced up at their approach and nervously set aside his comic book. He smoothed his red tie, which was stained with chocolate, and blinked behind his gold-rimmed glasses. He was probably only fifty years old, but his hair was snow white.

'Yes,' he said. 'Can I help you?'

'Yes,' Adam said. 'The two of us and two other friends were hiking in the hills behind Spooks . . .

*Spring*ville this morning when we came across these huge blocks of ice. We thawed one and this man – this cold man – jumped out and grabbed our friend, Watch. He dragged him into the woods, and we haven't seen Watch since.' Adam paused. 'We need your help to rescue him.'

The Chief just stared at him for a minute. Then he offered each of them his box of chocolates. 'Would you like one?' he asked.

'No thanks, we're not hungry,' Cindy said. 'We're too worried about our friend. Can you help us?'

The Chief helped himself to another chocolate. He ate it slowly, chewing seemed to take all his concentration.

'I don't know,' he said. 'What do you want me to help you with?'

Adam felt exasperated. 'We just told you. One of the Cold People kidnapped our friend. We want you to help us get him back.'

The Chief took off his glasses and cleaned them with a handkerchief. 'I'm alone here today. Do you really expect me to leave the station unattended?'

Cindy gestured to the empty building. 'Where are all the other police?'

The Chief seemed puzzled by the question. 'Well, I

don't very well know where they are. I can't keep track of everything. Years ago, when I started here, we had many fine officers, but their numbers have dwindled over time. Actually, I haven't seen another officer in the last few months.' He paused to think. 'It may have been in the last year.'

'But what do you do if there's an emergency?' Cindy asked.

'What am I supposed to do? I have problems of my own. I have to run this whole station all by myself. If I leave, what will become of it?'

'But you can't help anyone sitting in here,' Cindy said, annoyed. 'You just grow fat eating chocolates all day.'

The Chief was insulted. 'Watch your tongue young lady. I offered you a chocolate fair and square and you turned it down. Why shouldn't I eat it? If I don't, it will go to waste. There are a lot of hungry people in the world. Children in Africa are starving to death. I don't just throw away chocolates and pretend it's not wrong.'

'We're not talking about your chocolates,' Adam said, trying once more, although he was beginning to see that it was hopeless. 'We're talking about our friend. His life may be in danger. Can't you do anything to help him?'

The Chief leant over and peered at them. 'Does he have life insurance?'

'What?' Adam said. 'I don't know. What does that have to do with anything?'

The Chief smiled in a condescending manner. 'Young man, if he has insurance, and he is killed, his family will stand to gain financially. In these troubled times, extra income is nothing to take lightly. In other words, you view this as an emergency, but this might be a blessing in disguise. Certainly I would be doing your friend's family a disservice if I prevented them from receiving a large monetary settlement. So you see my hands are tied by my responsibilities to this station and my moral duty to this young man's family.'

'How can you talk about moral duty?' Cindy asked. 'When you're too much of a coward to lift a finger to save him?'

The Chief lost his smile. 'You call me a coward? You have a lot of nerve. Have I ever come to you for help to find one of my friends? Of course not. I attend to my own problems. You should do likewise, and quit bothering good people who just want to be left alone.'

'But you're a policeman,' Cindy said bitterly. 'It's your job to help people.'

That took the Chief back a step. He had to think for

a moment before answering. Before he did, however, he helped himself to another chocolate.

'There was nothing in my contract with the city that specified that I was to have to deal with mysterious Cold People,' he said. 'If there was, I would have had my lawyer strike it from my list of responsibilities. I don't even like the cold. That's another reason why I don't want to go outside today. I might catch a cold, and then where will this fine city be?'

'Probably no worse off,' Adam muttered. He turned towards the exit. 'Come, Cindy. Sally was right. We're wasting our time here.'

But Cindy was too frustrated to simply walk away. She walked up to the Chief's desk and suddenly reached out to grab his box of chocolates. Before he could stop her, she dropped it upside down on the dusty floor, ruining the contents. The Chief stared at her in shock but Cindy smiled sweetly.

'We have an emergency situation,' she said. 'Now you do too. How does it feel?'

Adam grabbed her arm and dragged her towards the door before the Chief could react. Adam was worried the man would throw her in jail.

'I think you've been hanging out with Sally too much,' Adam told her.

Five

The owner of the surplus store, Mr Patton, was dressed in full combat uniform. As Adam and Cindy entered his store, he was sitting on the floor and slipping bullets into a machine gun. He was approximately thirty-five, blond, muscled and hard like a marine. It looked like Bum and Sally had been talking to him about the Cold People. He wore a twisted grin. The battle he had been preparing for all his life had finally arrived.

'Welcome,' he said. 'Grab yourself a weapon and prepare to hit the front lines.'

'Our friends told you what's happening?' Adam asked.

'Sure did.' Mr Patton finished loading the machine gun. He jumped up and grabbed a grenade launcher from the shelf. 'The day of reckoning has finally arrived, like I always knew it would.'

'Excuse me,' Adam said. 'But I don't know if these creatures can be stopped by just bullets.'

Mr Patton flashed them a wild red-eyed look. 'That machine gun there is a M16. They were used in Nam – fire a sixteen bullet clip in less than five seconds. I get a lock on one of those creatures with that baby, I guarantee you the creature is going down.'

Adam shrugged. 'Well, I don't know much about guns.'

'I do,' Cindy said. 'My mother says they are disgusting and immoral.'

Mr Patton laughed. 'People always say those kind of things until real trouble shows up. You try stopping a bear with a white flag and it will have you for lunch. It's a jungle out there, I tell you.' He gestured towards the rear of the store. 'Your friends are in the back. I'm sure they agree with me. I think they're juicing up a couple of flame throwers.'

'I'm sure Sally would agree with you,' Adam said, stepping towards the back of the store.

'But she's crazy,' Cindy added.

They did find Sally and Bum at the back. Adam was surprised to see the store had its own supply of petrol. Sally and Bum were indeed fueling a couple of flame throwers and a couple of spare fuel tanks. The handheld weapons looked like portable rocket launchers, except they spouted fire rather than explosives. Sally already had one going, but with the power down low. The orange flame danced like a hyperactive lighter. Sally's eyes gleamed as she stared at the burning tip.

'Let them try to grab one of us now,' she said.

'Don't forget how fast they move,' Adam warned.

'*They?*' Cindy said. 'There's only one that's thawed out.'

'We have to figure they're all up and running around by now,' Bum said.

'Oh no,' Cindy moaned.

Adam was grim. 'I had figured as much myself.'

Sally smiled. 'How was the police station? Did you get lots of help?'

Adam shrugged. 'You were right. Don't rub it in.' He gestured to the flame throwers. 'Does Mr Patton only have two of them?'

'He has three but he's keeping one for himself,' Sally said. 'We can't complain. He gave us the easy payment plan on these two.'

'He actually believed the story about the Cold People?' Cindy asked.

'He'll believe any story about any kind of secret attack,' Bum said. 'It's what he lives for.'

Cindy checked her watch and grimaced. 'It's already two o'clock. Watch was taken at noon. I hope he's all right.'

'You heard what Bum said,' Sally snapped. 'We can't keep hoping he's fine. If we see him, we can't trust him. He's the enemy now.'

Cindy was shocked. 'How can you talk that way about our friend? I still have hope. I will keep hoping until this is all over. I don't care what anyone says.'

Sally went to snap back, then paused and drew in a deep breath. She momentarily closed her eyes. A spasm of pain crossed her face.

'I'm sorry,' she said softly. 'I have hope too.'

Adam had never heard Sally say she was sorry before.

He wasn't given a chance to ponder the wonder of the apology.

They heard a loud shout from the front of the store.

'They're coming!' Mr Patton cried. 'I see them down the road!'

As Bum had said, the army surplus store was not located in Spooksville proper, but on the outskirts. Between the store and the hills was nothing but a road and a field littered with clumps of bushes and rocks. As they rushed outside, they saw several blue-clad figures coming over the hills. Mr Patton had correctly identified them as Cold People because they were moving both stiffly and rapidly. There were six that Adam could see, but he had a feeling there were another half dozen just behind them. He was relieved that Watch wasn't with the group of monsters.

But otherwise he was more scared than he had ever been in his life.

Even from far away, the Cold People's eyes shone with a strange light.

'What do we do now?' Adam whispered.

Mr Patton shouldered his M16 and grenade launcher. 'It's party time, guys. Get your flame throwers ready. Let's head them off before they get into town. It's our day to be heroes.'

'Where's your flame thrower?' Adam asked.

'Inside the store,' Mr Patton said, already marching forward towards the advancing enemy. 'You can use it if you want. Just don't blow yourself up.'

'You should wait for us,' Bum said. 'We should attack together.'

Mr Patton waved him away. 'They're already dead meat. I don't need back-up.'

Bum turned to Adam. 'Get the other flame thrower. It's behind the counter. It's already fueled up. Hurry!'

Adam rushed inside and got the weapon. He was stunned by its weight. He had to drag it outside. He figured the fuel alone weighed ten kilos. The tip was already lit and it appeared easy to operate: if he squeezed the trigger, the flame grew longer.

Adam stepped back outside just in time to see Mr Patton raise his M16.

The surplus store owner took aim at the nearest Cryo creature.

Which just happened to be a beautiful woman.

'Take this you ice sucking monster!' Mr Patton screamed and fired.

He obviously did not have the weapon on rapid fire. He fired off only one bullet. He was an excellent shot: the bullet struck the woman in the centre of the chest. The round made an odd sound as it struck, like a bullet bouncing off a steel plate.

But it did not hurt her. There was no blood.

Not breaking stride, the woman kept coming. Yet the cold light in her eyes grew brighter. The shot had not hurt her but it had angered her. Mr Patton briefly lowered his weapon and shivered.

He was sixty metres away but Adam could see he was stunned.

'Don't stand still!' Sally yelled. 'She'll freeze you solid!'

Mr Patton appeared to hear Sally. Quickly he raised his M16 again. This time he let the whole clip of bullets fire. The amo tore at the woman's blue suit, but still it did not stop her. Mr Patton began to back away, dazed. Again Sally shouted at him.

'Try your grenade launcher!' she said.

'I think he should get back here,' Cindy said anxiously.

'We may already be trapped ourselves,' Bum said. 'Remember, we can't outrun them.'

Mr Patton turned and ran back towards them. But it was then the cold woman decided to chase after him. She was as fast as the man who had grabbed Watch. A glance over his shoulder showed Mr Patton that he would be caught before he could reach the store. Finally he took Sally's last piece of advice. Dropping to one knee, he raised the grenade launcher and took aim. To his credit, he kept his hands steady, something Adam doubted he would have been able to do with one of those monsters bearing down on him.

Mr Patton fired the grenade.

His aim was perfect. The grenade hit the woman's right shoulder.

There was a flash of fire, a loud bang.

The woman's right arm was gone. Shattered splinters.

The gang howled in delight.

'They can be stopped!' Sally yelled.

But Sally spoke too soon. The woman had lost an entire limb but there was no blood. In fact the wound did not even slow her down. Looking closer, Adam saw that her arm had cracked off the way it would have off an ice sculpture. Mr Patton had put a crack in her frozen armour, but he had not destroyed it. Adam suspected these creatures could keep coming with both their legs blown off. Certainly they could not bleed to death; they didn't have any blood.

The cold woman fell on Mr Patton.

He dropped his weapons and screamed.

They didn't stay to see what the creature did to him.

'Back in the store!' Bum yelled.

They raced to the surplus store and closed the door. They were in luck as far as the security of the place was concerned. The doors and windows not only had strong locks, but heavy metal grating. They pulled the steel bars over and snapped them shut just as the Cold

People reached the front door and pounded on it.
The door held. They were safe, for the moment.
But they were also trapped.

Six

In the gloom of the surplus store, they stared at each other, their faces pale with fear. The creatures outside continued to circle the building. They had cut off the power, the lights were out. The pounding on the front door had stopped but Adam knew the next attack would be much worse.

'What are we going to do?' Cindy whispered.

'We're not going to get out of here on foot,' Bum said. 'That's for sure. But we might not need to. Just before you guys showed up, Sally and me found a couple of hot air balloons in the back. They must be from the First World War. They were carefully packaged. I bet they will still work, if we can get them up on the roof and inflated.'

'But they can't get us in here,' Cindy said. 'Maybe we should just stay here until help arrives.'

Sally shook her head. 'No one's coming to save us. And you have to see they're not leaving. They'll get in here eventually.'

Adam peered through a crack in the window. 'I don't see Mr Patton. What do you think they did to him?'

'It's better not to think about it,' Bum said. 'Come, let's get these balloons out.'

The boxes the balloons came in were massive. Actually, there were four boxes per balloon. The balloon gondola and supporting ropes were packaged separately. There was also the wide-mouthed burner that went beneath the balloons, and which would allow them to control their height. At the moment, Adam just wanted to get in a balloon and fly away as far as possible.

But he was worried about his family: his mother and father and little sister. He wished he could call them to warn them to get out of town, but the Cold People had destroyed the telephone lines to the store as well. He prayed they weren't changed into monsters, although his little sister had been practising to be a monster since her second birthday.

They were fortunate that there was a strong ladder that led to the roof. Working together, they were able to get all the balloon boxes up there. They were also lucky that the sides of the surplus store were relatively smooth. The Cold People who prowled round outside were not able to get a handle on the walls and climb up on the roof.

Still, standing on the roof and looking down, Adam could see that the monsters were not giving up. Bum stood beside him as he scanned the area. There were maybe ten Cold People visible. But Adam suspected there were more than that already entering the town. Bum put his hand on Adam's shoulder.

'Sally and I can put the balloons together,' he said. 'Why don't you and Cindy go back down into the store and keep guard?'

'That sounds like a good idea,' Adam said.

'Keep your flame throwers ready.'

Adam nodded. 'Work fast. They're so strong. They're going to get in here and they know it.'

Sally worked better alone, and Cindy was happy to leave her and join Adam on guard duty. Happy may have been a poor word to describe Cindy's state of mind. Adam had seen her scared before, but never like this. In their minds, they could both still hear Mr Patton's screams. But there was still no sign of him. Cindy stayed close to his side as they prowled the narrow aisles of the store. The minutes went by.

'There's so many explosives in here,' Cindy whispered finally. 'If they do break in and we have to use our flame throwers, we'll probably blow ourselves up.'

'We have to be careful,' Adam agreed. He gestured to what looked like a box of dynamite. 'How did Mr Patton ever get this stuff? You'd think it would be illegal.'

'Everything is legal in Spooksville,' Cindy said weakly. The words seemed to choke in her throat. Her eyes filled with tears. Adam touched her side.

'What is it?' he asked.

She put her hand to her head. 'I keep thinking of Watch. I wish he were here with us. I wish we could take him with us in our balloons.'

Adam patted her on the back. 'I keep thinking of him too.'

Cindy wiped at her face. 'You must think I'm acting like a sissy. I don't usually cry. But since I've been here in this town, it's been one crisis after another.'

'Yeah. But at least you never get bored.'

Cindy forced a smile. 'That is one compensation.'

Again Adam gestured to the box of dynamite. 'I think we should load some of this into our balloons.

You never know when it may come in handy.'

'Why? You saw that the grenade didn't even stop the woman.'

Adam paused. 'I know that. I just have this feeling – I can't explain it. I think we might want this dynamite later on.' Adam bent over and studied the boxes. 'Here, there's fuses and detonators and everything. I want to haul some up on the roof. Will you be all right down here for a few minutes?'

Cindy glanced uneasily around in the shadows. 'Don't be gone too long.'

Adam was surprised when he got back up on the roof to see that Sally and Bum nearly had the balloons together. In reality there were not many parts to assemble. Bum even had one of them already filling with hot air. The burner was blasting away beneath the huge canopy as Adam walked over and set down his case of dynamite.

'We should be able to take off in a few minutes,' Bum said.

'Good,' Adam said. 'I want to take these explosives with us.'

Sally looked up from her work. She was hooking the ropes on to the balloon gondola, which would carry at least two of them aloft.

'The more firepower the better,' she said.

'How is it downstairs?' Bum asked.

Before Adam could answer, they heard Cindy scream. Adam realised he had left his flame thrower downstairs. He had needed both his hands free to lift the dynamite on to the roof. He raced towards the ladder. Bum and Sally moved to follow but Adam stopped them.

'Finish getting the balloons ready!' he yelled. 'I'll help Cindy!'

Adam hurried downstairs. It seemed darker in the store than it had a minute ago. He saw his flame thrower lying at the base of the ladder, where he had left it. The tip was still spouting a short flame. But he did not see his friend, nor did he hear her any more.

'Cindy!' he called as he picked up the flame thrower.

Off to his left, in the direction of the back door, he heard glass break.

'Adam!' Cindy shouted.

Relieved she could still respond, Adam ran towards her.

In the rear of the store, he found Cindy guarding a door that was about to cave in. As he feared, the Cold People were bending back the metal security bars. There were a total of four of them, all working on the

58

same door: two men and two women. One of the men was already squeezing his head through the bars. He was reaching for the lock.

'Shoot him!' Adam yelled as he ran up.

'I can't!' Cindy cried. 'I just can't burn someone!'

'If you don't they'll freeze you.' Adam pushed her out of the way and raised his flame thrower. The man took one look at the burning tip of the weapon and went to withdraw his head. Adam let fly a huge tongue of fire but it missed completely – the Cryo creature was that fast. But the wood round the door caught fire, which was not good. It made it easier for the door to collapse. Adam grabbed Cindy's hand. 'We have to get out of here!' he said.

They ran towards the steps that led to the roof. But just as Cindy put her foot on the first rung, the back door exploded in a shower of sharp glass and twisted metal. All four Cold People rushed in. They came at Adam like flying blocks of ice. He shoved Cindy in the back.

'Get up on the roof!' he shouted.

'You come too!' Cindy cried.

'Give me a second,' Adam said. With Cindy running up the ladder, he raised the flame thrower and squeezed the trigger hard. The stream of flame that flew out was huge; it caused the Cold People to scatter. Then another two monsters burst through the ruined back door. Adam realised he could not hold them off for ever. He stepped on to the ladder and started up the steps.

He was almost to the roof when something cold grabbed his right ankle.

Adam tripped and fell.

Sprawled over the steps, he turned to see a Cryo creature below him.

Blue ice-like fingers were wrapped round Adam's foot.

The creature tightened its grip.

Adam felt its nails go into his skin.

He saw blood – his blood. It stained his white socks red.

Adam gasped and raised his flame thrower. But he could not shoot the monster straight in the face, not unless he wanted to fry his own foot. For a second he didn't know what to do. Blood continued to stain his sock.

The creature began to pull him down.

Its eyes shone with cold light.

Adam decided he could stand a little burn.

He fired the flame thrower. But he aimed high,

above the creature's head and away from his bleeding foot. The heat of the fire, however, was enough to force the monster to jerk back. Adam was able to pull his foot free. But the monster was quick to recover. Once more it reached out with its freezing claw. But this time Adam was ready for it.

He shot the monster right in the face.

For a second the creature's head was a ball of pure flame.

Adam heard a weird scream. It was thin and high-pitched; the sound an alien bat might make as it died. Perhaps the Cold People were like evil vampires, Adam thought, that spread by stealing human blood and replacing it with cryo fluid. The scream pierced Adam's chest and made his heart shiver.

But the monster's face did not burn.

Rather, it seemed to blur. Its features ran together. It was a ball of wax thrown into a simmering oven. The eyes seeped into the nose. The mouth dissolved into the chin. Its powerful hands seemed to reach up to hold the parts in place, but the moment they entered the flames, they too began to melt. Adam watched in horror and amazement. The creature toppled backwards, and fell down the stairs.

It landed in a disfigured pile at the foot of the ladder.

The other Cryo creatures gathered round.

They stared down at their headless partner.

Then up at Adam. Their eyes turned *very* cold.

Adam felt hands on him, trying to pull him up on to the roof.

'We're ready to take off!' Sally yelled. 'Leave them!'

'I'm coming,' Adam said as he limped up the remainder of the ladder.

But once on the roof, rather than running towards the waiting balloons, Adam turned back to the ladder and locked the flame thrower trigger on high. It was a shame to leave the weapon behind, but he was determined to even up the score for what they had done to Watch, and then some. With the weapon gushing fire, he threw it down into the store. The creatures scattered as it landed beside their fallen comrade. Adam noted the direction of the spouting flame.

It was pointed toward Mr Patton's ammunition supplies.

Adam ran towards one of the waiting balloons.

He heard loud explosions below. More high-pitched screams.

Adam limped as he ran.

His injured ankle was turning strangely numb.

Seven

Adam ended up in the balloon with Sally. Cindy was with Bum. They floated off the roof and were dragged away from the surplus store by a gust of north wind. Their escape came none too soon. Two Cryo creatures piled on to the roof. One leapt to catch Adam and Sally's balloon, and barely missed. Sally hung over the side and shot at it with her flame thrower.

'Just so it doesn't think of trying again,' she said. She had missed.

'They're not safe on that roof,' Adam muttered as the building fell away.

'What do you mean?' Sally asked.

'Just watch,' Adam said.

The grand finale came quickly. The two monsters were trying to climb back down the ladder when a river of flame shot up at them, and they were turned into melting torches. They staggered on the roof before toppling off the sides. There followed a series of crushing bangs and the entire rear of the store disintegrated. Finally, even as one creature tried to run out the front door, there was a single massive explosion, and the store was engulfed in flame. Mr Patton may not have sold that many exotic weapons in his days, but they had done the job when they were needed. Sally smiled in wonder.

'I think you got all of them,' she said.

Adam shook his head and slumped to the floor of the balloon gondola. He rubbed his right ankle. The wound was superficial; the bleeding had stopped. But he didn't seem able to get the circulation going in it.

'We got maybe eight of them,' he said. 'I think there's dozens more.'

Sally noticed his bloody sock and knelt beside him. 'Are you hurt? Are you in pain?'

'No. The creature barely dug his nails in. But . . .'

'What?' Sally asked.

'I don't know. My foot's numb. I can hardly stand on it.'

Sally drew back anxiously. 'Maybe when it grabbed you it injected cryo fluid into your system. Maybe it's going to circulate throughout your body and transform you into one of those horrible monsters. Soon you will start frothing at the mouth and crave human blood.'

'Thank you, Sally,' Adam said flatly. 'You have an amazing way of making a guy feel good when things are not going well. Now I suppose you want to change places with Cindy in the other balloon?'

'Well . . .' Sally said.

'I'll throw you overboard if you don't stop,' Adam warned.

Sally moved to his side and squeezed the flesh above his ankle. 'Don't worry, I won't leave you. Can you feel that?'

'Yes. Sort of. I feel like . . .' Adam trailed off.

'The numb sensation is going up your leg?' Sally asked.

Adam hesitated. 'Yes.'

Sally looked worried. 'We need to get you to a doctor.'

'The only doctor that could help me lived back in Mu.' Adam paused and swallowed thickly. He had to face the reality of the situation. 'I might need to have my lower leg amputated. Before it spreads all the way.'

'In this town you don't need a doctor for that. Just get down on the jetty and hang your leg in the water. A shark will bite it off for you.'

Adam hung his head. 'Thanks a lot. You wouldn't say that if it were your leg.'

Sally leant over and hugged him. 'You know I really am worried. But maybe it's not as bad as it seems. Maybe the numbing sensation will wear off.'

'I hope so,' Adam said quietly.

'Hey, what's going on over there?' Cindy called from the other balloon which was floating only ten metres away. Sally stood up to answer.

'None of your business,' she called.

'Where's Adam?' Bum asked.

Sally glanced down at him. 'He's resting. He's had a hard day.' She added, 'But don't worry. He's not turning into an alien monster.'

Cindy and Bum looked at each other.

'Adam,' Cindy said. 'Are you sure you're all right?'

Adam struggled to his feet. 'Yeah. I just twisted my ankle, that's all.'

'He doesn't have a strange infection or anything,' Sally said.

'Would you shut up,' Adam whispered to her.

'What?' Sally whispered back. 'I'm not saying anything.'

'The day you don't say anything, the sky will crack open and angels will appear.'

'That happened here once,' Sally said.

'What do we do now?' Cindy called over.

Adam stared in the direction of town. They appeared to be drifting that way. He didn't see any more Cold People but he realised that meant nothing.

'Right now we're at the mercy of the wind,' Adam called back. 'At least it decides which way we're going. But using the burner we can rise high or sink lower. If we fly over some Cold People we might want to drop down and try to fry them with our flame throwers.'

'But soon people in town will be changed,' Bum warned them. 'Are we going to try to melt them as well?'

'There are some people in town I wouldn't mind melting,' Sally muttered.

'We'll cross that bridge when we come to it,' Adam said.

They didn't exactly come to a bridge, but they did drift towards the cemetery and Ann Templeton's castle. Even from a distance they could see a lot going on there. As they drew closer, they saw over a dozen Cold People circling the witch's home. The Cold People seemed to be laying siege to the place. Perhaps they knew of her great powers. Ann Templeton had withdrawn the bridge that crossed her moat. Vaguely, through the surrounding trees, Adam could see strange creatures manning the walls and stone windows of the castle. The Cold People appeared to be trying to fell a huge fallen tree so that they could cross the moat and invade the place. Over in the other balloon, Bum laughed at their efforts.

'They're not going to get to her,' Bum said. 'I'd bet everything I own on it.'

'Yeah, but you're a bum,' Sally said. 'You don't own anything.'

'Just watch,' Bum said. 'She'll give them a scare.'

Bum knew his witch. Just as the Cold People toppled the tree into the moat and prepared to cross, a bright flash of fire stabbed from the top tower of the castle. There was a loud cracking sound, like a bolt of lightning. The tree burst into fire and several of the Cold People plunged into the water.

'There's crocodiles in that moat,' Bum said.

Again, he was right. Even as they watched, the Cold People in the water were attacked from below. Sally let out a cheer.

'They're falling faster than we thought they would!' she said.

But she spoke too soon. A couple of Cold People sunk beneath the surface, but they came back up quickly. And in their hands they each held a crocodile by the neck. The friends watched in horror as the monsters snapped the huge reptiles in half. The moat water turned a dark red.

'I don't believe this,' Cindy cried.

Another blast of fire shot down from the high tower. It hit the water and there was an explosion of steam. The Cold People retreated back to the shore, away from the castle. Clearly they were driven off, but none of them was destroyed.

Adam said it for all of them: 'They might not be able to get to the witch,' he said, 'but she can't get out of her castle.'

Bum agreed. 'I think this is one battle we will have to fight without her help.' Bum stopped and peered into the cemetery which was now directly below them. Excitedly, he pointed to a tombstone, in the corner of the graveyard. 'Is that Watch?'

Eight

It was definitely their friend.

Watch seemed dazed. He wandered about the tombstones as if looking for his own place of burial. His clothes were slightly torn – round the collar, at the hem of his trousers. But he still had on his four watches and his thick glasses. He seemed not to notice them, although they were not far above, maybe thirty metres. Adam couldn't help noticing how pale his skin was.

'We have to save him,' Cindy called over softly.

'That may not be a good idea,' Bum said. 'He might be beyond saving.'

Sally turned to Adam. 'What do you want to do?' she asked gently.

Adam felt choked with sorrow. 'I sure don't want to leave him down there with all those monsters. But . . .'

'Yeah?' Sally said. 'But what?'

Adam shook his head. 'You know the situation. What do you think?'

Sally peered down into the cemetery. Watch had stopped and was just staring off into empty space. His eyes, seen through his thick glasses, appeared normal. But he was not standing as he usually did.

'There's something wrong with him,' Sally said finally.

'I don't care,' Cindy said. 'He's still our friend. We can't abandon him.'

'Not so loud,' Sally warned. 'He might hear us.'

'We might want to call down to him,' Bum said. 'See how he reacts.'

'No,' Adam said. 'If we shout to him, the other Cold People might hear too. At least right now, if we want to rescue him, he's alone.'

'It's risky,' Bum said. 'We don't know how strong he is now. He could destroy us all.'

Adam was grim. 'Yeah. And we can't use our flame throwers on him.'

'But if he's changed,' Sally said, 'he might not know that we used to be his friends. He won't know that we won't try to fry him. If we surround him, we might be able to knock him out and then tie him up. We have extra rope.'

'We're not going to hurt him,' Cindy said.

'We might have to hurt him a little to help him,' Sally snapped at her. 'This is an emergency situation. Stop behaving like a self righteous little princess. We have to harden our hearts.'

'If it were you I wouldn't mind picking up a bat,' Cindy said.

'You would just end up clobbering yourself,' Sally retorted.

'All right, all right,' Adam said, wanting to stop them from getting into a long argument. 'We'll drop down and see how he is. If he attacks, we'll try to knock him unconscious.'

'If we take him with us,' Bum said. 'What are we going to do when he regains consciousness?'

'We'll worry about that later,' Adam said.

'That's what the scientists who built the first atomic bomb would say to each other when someone asked "what if we blow up the world?" ' Sally muttered.

Dropping down was easy. All they had to do was vent off some of their hot air. Watch continued to stand staring off into the distance. Because the castle was next to the cemetery, the other Cold People were not far away, about half a kilometre. It would take a miracle for them not to see the balloons. For that reason Adam knew they had to act fast. He worried that they might be making a huge mistake. But he figured if he had to risk his life, it should be for his friend.

They landed in a small clearing in the cemetery, thirty metres behind Watch's back. Still, incredibly, he appeared unaware of them. They had two flame throwers left. Sally took one, Bum the other as they climbed out of the balloon gondolas. Adam searched the ground for a strong stick, and found one that fitted his grip.

But Adam limped as he walked.

The numbing sensation was definitely climbing.

As a group, they approached Watch cautiously.

Watch continued to stand before a huge tombstone.

Adam realised it was Madeline Templeton's.

The tomb was at the end of the Secret Path.

A portal into other dimensions.

Was Watch in such pain, Adam wondered, that he was thinking of fleeing into another reality? It was horrible to think of his friend possessed with the evil spirit of the Cryo creatures.

But it was not as horrible as having to stare into his friend's face.

Watch suddenly whirled on them.

His eyes shone with a cold light.

His mouth twisted in an evil line.

A painfully high-pitched wail tore past his lips.

Then he attacked.

Adam – although lame – led the group and was therefore closest to Watch. He was the first one to suffer the brunt of Watch's new found power. With his bad foot, he just couldn't move fast enough to get out of Watch's way. He felt as if he had been rammed by a freight train when Watch crashed into him. For a second, Adam went flying through the air. He dropped his stick. He only stopped when he ran into a bigger stick – a tree, actually. It hurt to smash into the trunk, but Adam was back up in an instant, numb leg or not.

The situation was already desperate and the fight was only three seconds old. As Adam's vision cleared, he saw that Cindy had also been knocked down. She may have been hit harder; she did not get up right away. Bum and Sally were still safe, for the moment, behind their flame throwers. But they were doing nothing to corner Watch. On the contrary, Watch was driving them further apart. Because they would not fire, they had only the tiny flames at the tip of the flame throwers to scare him with. And Watch did not look that scared.

'Shoot off more fire,' Adam said. 'Let him know he can be burned.'

'Good idea,' Sally agreed, as she pulled back on her trigger. The tongue of flame stretched out a metre and Watch quickly withdrew from attacking her. He turned to Bum instead, who also lengthened his flame. For the first time, Watch took a step back. Adam grabbed the stick he had dropped and limped forward.

'Drive him against the wall,' Adam said. 'We can only capture him if we corner him.'

'Do we want to capture him?' Bum asked again as he pushed Watch back with the flame. 'We won't be able to control him.'

'We can do what Sally said,' Adam replied. 'We can tie him up.'

'I don't know if rope can hold him,' Sally said, having second thoughts.

'Just get him against the wall,' Adam ordered.

A minute after they started on the offensive, Watch was cornered against the tall wall. He glared at them with his weird glowing eyes and they each felt a chill. But he did not have the power of the original Cryo creatures. He could make them shiver, but he could not freeze them where they stood.

'Now what?' Sally demanded.

'Now I'll talk to him,' Adam said, taking a wobbly step forward.

'What are you going to talk about?' Sally asked. 'Ice-cream? Popsicles? The guy is a walking ice-cube. You can't talk to him.'

Adam gripped his stick tightly. 'A part of him must remember us.'

'We'll keep guard,' Bum said. 'But if he does attack, we may have to burn him a little.'

'I understand,' Adam said. 'Try not to burn me while you're at it.'

Adam stepped to within two metres of Watch. His friend had his back pressed against the wall. He continued to glare at them, although something in his eyes seemed to change as he stared at Adam. There may have been a flicker of recognition. Adam could not be sure, but it gave him hope.

'Watch,' Adam said. 'We don't want to hurt you. We want to help you. Do you remember me, Watch? I'm Adam. I'm your friend.'

Watch stopped glaring and his right cheek twitched. The weird light in his eyes faded, although his eyes did not return to normal. There was a blankness to them Adam found disturbing. It was as if Watch's brain had been wiped clean by the Cryo creature. Once again,

Adam wondered if he could ever be changed back to normal.

'I really am your friend, Watch,' Adam said, encouraged by the change, any change, in his condition. Adam took another step forward and held out his hand. 'You can come with us. We'll take you away from these evil monsters.'

At the mention of the word monsters Watch glanced in the direction of the castle. So far the other Cold People had not appeared. But Adam knew their luck could not last for ever. Watch's dull expression seemed to tremble with pain as he looked in the direction of his new partners. For a moment he appeared terribly sad. Adam took another step towards him. Watch was now just over a metre away.

'Please try to remember,' Adam pleaded. 'Your name is Watch. You're a human being.'

For a second Watch's dull expression vanished.

He smiled faintly. Adam smiled brightly.

'Watch!' Adam cried. He dropped his stick and moved to hug his friend.

But the smile faded. The cold light returned.

Watch leapt towards Adam, his fingers spread like claws.

Again, Adam felt a terrible blow and went down.

Through a fog of physical and emotional pain, he saw Watch raise his claws to rip into his chest and pull out his heart and fill his body with cryo fluid. But before Watch could strike again, Adam also saw the blur of a brown stick as it was brought down on the back of Watch's head. His friend blinked and the wicked light in his eyes went out. Watch toppled to the side.

'He has a hard head,' Sally said, setting aside the stick Adam had dropped. Adam noticed that the stick had broken in the middle. Sally must have hit Watch pretty hard. He lay sprawled on his back. He did not appear to be breathing. Adam knelt anxiously by his side.

'Is he dead?' he moaned.

Bum shook his head. 'Cryo creatures don't breathe. I don't even know if their hearts beat.'

'Is he all right?' Cindy called, staggering over, a hand to her head.

'He's unconscious,' Adam said. 'But we think he's still alive. How are you?'

'She looks terrible,' Sally muttered.

Cindy snorted in Sally's direction. 'You take the kind of hit I did and we'll see how long you stay down.' She nodded to Watch. 'Let's get him in one of the balloons.'

'I don't like this,' Bum said as he leant over and picked up Watch. 'But if we're going to take him, we better take him now.' He nodded in the direction of the castle. 'I think they heard us. They're coming.'

Bum was right – four of the Cold People were climbing the cemetery walls. The monsters had three times as far to go to get to the balloons, but Adam wondered who was going to get there first. His ankle seemed to be getting worse with each passing second. It was now almost completely numb, and the cold sensation was as high up as his right knee. He fell behind the others as they raced for the balloons. He wondered if he would be joining Watch soon – as a monster.

Sally reached the balloons first, of course, and began to loosen the ropes that would allow them to take off.

'Hurry!' Sally screamed. 'Adam!'

Cindy arrived next at the balloons, followed by Bum who was still carrying Watch. But Adam was now tripping every other step. As he climbed back up, he saw that he was already too late. One of the Cold People had moved inbetween him and the balloons. He was trapped in a cemetery more dangerous than a snake pit. Adam froze as the Cryo creature – it was a woman with long white hair – fixed him with her gaze and slowly began to approach.

'Get away!' he called to the others. 'Save yourselves!'

'Drop that hero garbage!' Sally called back, climbing out of her balloon with her flame thrower ready. So intent was the cold woman on Adam, that she hardly seemed to notice Sally.

Until Sally torched her from behind.

She really gave it to her, turning the juice up high. Like the creature in the surplus store, the woman did not burn. It was more like the creature melted into a pile of sick blue fluid. Sally kept the flame blazing until there was nothing left of her except a smelly puddle sitting atop an old grave. Sally grabbed Adam by the arm and pulled him towards one of the balloons.

'I just hope I never have to do that to Watch,' she said, adding, 'or to you.'

Nine

They floated up and out of the cemetery before any more Cold People could get them. Adam was with Sally again. Bum had not placed Watch in his own balloon; Adam and Sally had him as well. Their friend lay sprawled on his back on the floor of the gondola. Sally knelt at Watch's feet, tying his ankles together. Adam sat on the floor of the gondola as well. He didn't know if he could stand again without support. The exercise in the cemetery had done nothing to drive away the numbness.

'I wish you didn't have to do that,' Adam said to Sally.

She began to knot the rope. 'Just wait till he wakes up and we'll see what you wish.'

Adam put his hand on top of Watch's head.

It was like touching a block of ice.

'It's like he's dead,' Adam said.

'Maybe it would be better if he was.'

Adam was shocked. 'How can you say that?'

Sally lowered her head. 'I just have to look at him. He's not Watch any more.'

'But you saw him just before he attacked. For a second he recognised me.'

Sally nodded sadly. 'I saw it. I hope it means something.' She sighed and stood to look out over the city. 'We're drifting toward the centre of town. I think I see more Cold People below us.'

Adam clawed his way up and leaned on the side. He was stunned to see three Cold People run into a house directly below them and drag a man and woman out on to the lawn screaming. The Cold People pinned the couple down on the grass. Adam had to look away. He could not bear to see how the monsters made more of themselves. The couple's screams echoed in his ears as he slouched back down beside Watch.

'We can't just float around up here all day,' he said. 'We have to take more aggressive action.'

Sally sat beside him. 'We're probably not going to get another situation like we had at the surplus store where we were able to cook a bunch of them all at once.

I think the best we can do is swoop down every now and then to fry one or two of them.'

'That's no good,' Adam said. 'Especially since they're now going to make more of their kind every few minutes. We have to do something that will wipe them all out at once.' Adam pounded his numb leg lightly with his clenched fist. 'What is it that they're afraid of besides fire?'

Sally was thoughtful. 'We haven't seen anything else. We know bullets and grenades can't stop them.'

A remarkable idea occurred to Adam. 'Wait a second! We asked ourselves earlier why they appeared today. We thought the cold weather had something to do with it.'

'Yeah. We guessed that they might have even changed the weather.'

'Yes, exactly,' Adam said. 'They probably did. It's summer and it's freezing today. That's an incredible coincidence. But what we didn't ask ourselves is *why* they would have changed the weather.'

Sally shrugged. 'They probably like the cold.'

'No,' Adam said. 'They probably *need* the cold. There's a big difference between liking something and needing it. I wonder if it got warmer if they would all begin to die. Remember Bum's story. When Atlantis attacked Mu, the Cryo creatures dashed up to the north pole.'

'So they wouldn't be killed by the nuclear blasts,' Sally said.

'If they were just worried about the blasts, they could have gone anywhere else. But they didn't go anywhere else. I think they fled to the north pole because all the bombs – and the asteroid – raised the temperature of the whole world. It's possible they *had* to go to the north pole.'

'What's your point?' Sally asked. 'We don't have any nuclear bombs here. Or asteroids. We can't just change the weather.'

Adam sat up straighter. He could feel the power of his idea. He was sure he was on to something important.

'A couple of weeks ago we were having an argument about the witch,' he said. 'You were complaining about how rich she was, and how she never shared her wealth. You also said she was wrecking the local environment. Do you remember?'

'Yes. So what?'

'You said the worst thing she ever did – besides murdering hundreds of innocent children – was to drill several huge oil wells in the hills behind Spooksville. I remember how you said they were somewhere above the reservoir.'

Sally paused. 'What are you saying?'

'The reservoir supplies the water for all of Spooksville. It also has many underground streams that lead away from it and flow under the entire city. We've heard them before when we've been up there. When we were trapped in the Haunted Cave, we even saw one of those streams.'

'Say what you have to say. You're driving me crazy.'

'Don't you see?' Adam said. 'If we can divert the oil that's being pumped out of the ground at the witch's wells, we can flood the reservoir with tons of oil. And if we're able to ignite that oil, we will have the biggest fire this area has seen in the last ten thousand years. The local temperature will soar.'

'Up in the hills,' Sally protested. 'Not so much down here.'

'You're wrong. You're forgetting what I said about the underground streams. The water in them will heat as well. It will boil, and it will heat the ground. If we can get enough oil, if we can cause the whole reservoir to burn, we can drive the temperature back up to where we're all sweating.'

Sally considered for a long time. 'It's not easy to

ignite crude oil that's been mixed with water. You need something powerful to trigger the fuel.'

Adam patted the box of dynamite that rested beside them. 'What do you think I brought this for?'

Sally was amazed. 'You didn't have this idea back at the surplus store?'

Adam shook his head. 'No. I just had this feeling . . . I can't explain it. Maybe there is such a thing as intuition.'

Sally nodded. 'I like this plan. I like big fires. But we're going to have trouble making it all work. The wind decides the course of this balloon. We're going to have to land, and we're going to need transportation up to the hills – fast transportation.' Sally paused. 'We need a jeep. Something that can climb through hills.'

'But we don't know how to drive.'

'Speak for yourself. I learned to drive in kindergarten.'

'But you don't have a driver's licence,' Adam said.

'I think that's the least of our worries right now.' Sally gestured to Watch. 'We shouldn't take him with us. He might ruin the whole plan.'

'I don't want to leave him helpless while all that trouble is going on below us.'

'I understand,' Sally said. 'But if we do get a

jeep, we're locking him in the trunk.'

'Do jeeps have trunks?' Adam asked.

'We'll find one that does.' Sally stood. 'We need to tell the others about our plan.'

'You can tell them you thought it up if you like.'

'I was going to do that anyway,' she replied.

Ten

They did not spot a jeep, but a large four-wheel drive truck with a camper shell on the back. They decided not to be choosy. The city below was turning to chaos. The Cold People had invaded the local shopping centre. People were running and screaming everywhere. Plus, Adam and Sally now began to see a new horror. Many of the people the Cryo creatures had first grabbed were now going after those who had not been changed. Adam figured by sunset it would be all over, at least as far as Spooksville was concerned.

Unless the plan worked.

On the floor of the balloon gondola, Watch continued to lie still.

'I wish some of these panicking people would light a few fires,' Sally said as they began to descend towards the truck. 'They don't know anything about rioting.'

'It's not a skill you can practise,' Adam said.

'How are you going to start the truck without keys?' Cindy called from the other balloon. Bum was making it descend so that he and Cindy could help guard the other two while they moved Watch and the dynamite into the truck.

'I'm going to hot-wire it,' Sally said.

'Who taught you how to do that?' Adam asked.

'I did,' Bum said. 'You never know when the skill will come in handy.' He added, 'Like right now.'

'How are you going to even get into the truck without keys?' Cindy asked.

'What are all these stupid questions?' Sally snapped impatiently. 'We are trying to save the world here, Cindy, in case you hadn't noticed. I will take a big rock and break the window if I have to.'

'I was just asking,' Cindy muttered.

'You might want to land on top of the truck,' Bum said. 'It will give you some protection.'

'I was thinking the same thing,' Adam replied. Although the balloon could not really be steered, it could be manoeuvred slightly by tightening and loosening the ropes that supported the balloon itself. Adam had already lowered the burner and vented a lot of hot air. They were going down pretty fast. The street the truck was parked on looked like a war zone.

Adam was barely able to hold himself up by hanging on to the side of the gondola. His right leg, up to his mid thigh, was completely numb. He would not be able to walk without hanging on to Sally. He would not be able to transfer the dynamite or move Watch. Sally would have to do everything. He hated feeling so helpless.

'I really think you guys should take Watch,' Sally said when they were only fifteen metres above the truck. 'We don't need anything that might slow us down.'

'We'll both have to land to transfer him,' Bum said. 'That could be dangerous.'

'It might not be a good idea to move him while he's unconscious,' Cindy added.

Sally snorted and spoke to Adam. 'They just don't want him. They're afraid of him. Oh well, I guess you see who your friends really are when you've been transformed into a monster.'

'You know, you have been a pain in the butt all day,' Cindy said.

Sally laughed. 'I am one of mankind's last hopes for salvation. I have the right to be a pain in the butt.'

Cindy looked at Bum.

'She does have a point there,' Bum said.

'Get ready,' Adam said. 'We're directly above the truck. I'm going to dump more hot air. We'll drop like a rock.'

They did not exactly drop like a rock, but they came down hard. Watch seemed to stir as a result of the jolt. Adam was the only one to notice. Sally was already out of the gondola and trying to break into the car. It was Adam's turn to hold the flame thrower. If a Cryo creature so much as looked their way, he was turning up the heat.

Cindy and Bum floated fifteen metres overhead.

'Make sure you have gas in the truck,' Bum called down. 'It's a long drive up to the wells.'

'I hope we don't have to stop for service,' Sally called back. She had tried the door and it was locked. Picking up a nearby brick, she smashed the driver's window and unlocked the door. Opening the door, she brushed away the big pieces of glass. She didn't have time to worry about the tiny shards. She would probably cut her butt on the way up to the hills. Just what she needed.

Adam handed her the case of dynamite as she jumped back on top of the truck. That was no problem to deposit on the front seat of the truck, but when she returned for Watch, and Adam, she wondered how she was going to help them both into the truck.

'You won't be able to lift Watch over the side of the gondola,' Adam said. 'And I won't be able to help you lift him. So what we're going to have to do is burn a hole in the side of it. Then you can just pull Watch out and slide him down.' Adam gestured for her to stand back. 'I'll try not to start a major fire.'

Adam half kept his promise. He blasted away a large chunk of the gondola and Sally was able to slide Watch out and stuff him in the truck's camper. She locked him inside, in fact. Unfortunately, the gondola continued to burn and the flames went into the balloon itself. Adam was barely able to get clear before the hot air caused by the fire shot the balloon into the sky.

It flew right by Bum and Cindy, before self-destructing in a ball of flame.

'I hate to see it go,' Sally said to Adam as she helped him into the passenger's side. 'It saved our lives a couple of times.'

'When this is all over we'll go for a real balloon ride,' Adam said. He dragged his lifeless leg into the truck, shut the door and rolled down the window. Cradling the flame thrower on his lap, he leant out of the window and signalled to Cindy and Bum to get away. 'Try to help people where you can,' he called.

Bum shook his head. 'You guys are our only hope.'

'Good luck!' Cindy called.

'Bless you!' Sally called back sarcastically before climbing in the truck. She took one look at the truck's gears and groaned. 'Oh no.'

'What's the matter?' Adam asked, the box of dynamite sitting between them.

'It's a stick shift. I learnt on an automatic.'

'What's the difference?'

'What do you mean what's the difference? I know how to drive one type. I don't know how to drive the other.'

'Well, you're just going to have to learn,' Adam said.

'That's easy for you to say. How come you don't know how to drive?'

'Because I'm twelve years old and I'm originally from a normal town in the midwest where they don't teach twelve year olds to drive. Now would you quit complaining and just get us out of here. This street isn't exactly a safe place to talk, in case you didn't notice.'

'I'll try. That's all a girl can do.' Sally pulled up the seat so her feet could reach to the pedals. It was fortunate Sally's legs were as long as they were, or else they would have had to steal a motorcycle. Next she lifted up the brick she had used to smash the window.

Bringing it down on the ignition switch – and breaking it – she pulled out a couple of red and yellow wires. When she touched them the engine roared to life and the truck leapt forward.

Then the engine stalled.

'Why did that happen?' Adam demanded. 'Are we out of gas?'

'No. I think I need to start with the truck in neutral.'

'Then do that,' Adam snapped.

'I will! I just happen to be going through a tough learning curve right now. Give me a second.' Sally pressed in one of the pedals on the floor and shifted the gears into neutral. Again she touched the wires together. The engine started and the truck began to roll forward. Sally shifted the gears once more – this time into first gear – and the truck picked up speed. 'I'm a genius!' Sally exclaimed.

They ran into a fire hydrant.

The water exploded like a geyser.

It drenched their roof. They could have been in a storm.

'What kind of genius are you?' Adam asked.

'The kind that doesn't respond well to criticism.' Sally shifted into reverse. 'Fasten your seat-belt and don't say another word.'

Eleven

Ten minutes after saying goodbye to Adam and Sally, Cindy and Bum began to feel guilty about not doing more to help their friends. At least Cindy felt guilty. She didn't know if guilt was an emotion Bum allowed himself to experience.

'Maybe we should have gone with them,' she said as they floated towards the beach. The invasion was sweeping through the whole town. The sounds of screaming were unimaginable and heart-rending. Cindy kept putting her hands over her ears and eyes. But she could not block out what was happening. What she wanted to do more than anything in the whole world was rescue her mother and her younger brother, Neil. But she wondered if that was a selfish thought. Bum was right – their real hope lay with Adam and Sally.

'I don't know if we could have helped them that way,' Bum said.

'But we're not doing anybody any good up here,' Cindy protested.

Bum gestured. 'Will we do any good getting transformed into Cryo creatures?'

Cindy searched for the ruined lighthouse which was not far from her home. But they were at least five kilometres north of her street. If they landed, and she did manage to fight through to her house and reach her mother and brother, the balloon would surely not be there when she got back.

'I wish we had found a helicopter in the surplus store,' she said, frustrated. 'Not being able to steer this thing is driving me crazy.'

Bum scratched his unshaven face. 'I've been thinking about that very problem. There might be a solution. Coming up below us is a hardware store. You can see it there beside those trees. They carry large fans. We might be able to rig one up and use it for propulsion and to steer.'

'What would we use to power it? We can't plug it in.'

'There are portable generators in the store. They run on petrol. We could drain some fuel out of our flame thrower. We wouldn't need much. The largest fan would only need a small generator to power it.'

Cindy liked the idea. 'Where would we head?'

Bum spoke gently. 'I know you have family in town. We could try to rescue them.' He added, 'If that's what you want.'

Cindy looked down at the madness. Sally was finally getting her wish. Several fires had broken out. Homes and cars alike were burning. And to think of her mother and brother down there. It was too painful for Cindy to contemplate.

'Let's get the fan and the generator,' she whispered. 'Then we can decide.'

Bum was becoming an expert at ballooning. He brought them down right on top of the hardware store. He anchored their flying machine by tying one of its ropes to a roof vent. He offered to let her carry the flame thrower but she declined.

'At the surplus store I found I couldn't burn someone,' she said.

'We're all lucky Sally doesn't have your inhibitions,' Bum said.

Cindy nodded. 'She's a brave girl. I admire her for that quality.' She added, 'I just never tell her that.'

They found a way into the hardware store's attic.

From there they had no trouble getting down to the main level. The place was deserted, and they supposed that was a good thing. But Cindy found the silent aisles spooky. She kept thinking something was going to jump out at them. Bum steered them in the direction of the fans.

'Look, they're on sale,' Bum said as they reached the right department. 'That's a big break. I haven't cashed my pay cheque.'

'How do you survive out on the streets without money?'

'I rely upon my charm and good looks.'

'No, really. I often wonder how you eat. Where you sleep.'

Bum spoke seriously. 'Cindy. Mankind has existed on this planet for centuries before the invention of money. Dollar bills and credit cards do not make the world go round, as most people think. I was rich at one time and now I'm poor. But I have to say, I'm a lot happier owning nothing than owning tons of stuff I still have to pay for. Does that make sense?'

Cindy chuckled. 'It makes perfect sense.'

They studied the fans, trying to figure out which one would suit them best. They ended up selecting two large round ones that came with stands. Their choice of generators was also easy. There were only two types: a big one and a small one. The big one was for powering heavy equipment. They took the small one.

They were loading the equipment beside the ladder that led into the attic, and from there to the roof, when they were attacked.

The creature seemed to come out of nowhere.

He grabbed Bum from behind, and lifted him off his feet.

Bum was squeezed tight.

He dropped the flame thrower. It clanged at his feet.

'Cindy!' Bum shouted. 'Help!'

Cindy froze in terror when she saw what was happening. This creature did not wear a blue jump suit. This was not one of the original Cryo creatures. Like Watch, this man had started out the day a normal human being. But now he was the enemy. As Cindy stood stunned, the thing began to drag Bum away. It was strong. Bum fought and kicked but couldn't break loose.

'The flame thrower,' Bum gasped as he was yanked round the corner. 'Cindy.'

By a sheer act of will, Cindy broke her paralysis. She grabbed the flame thrower and chased after Bum and the creature. For a man who had just been changed into a monster, he sure moved fast. She only caught up with them as the creature was about to drag Bum outside. She raised the flame thrower, pulling back slightly on the trigger. The flame moved out a foot.

'Let go of him or you burn!' she shouted.

This creature wasn't totally stupid. It understood what fire was, and it knew that it could use Bum as a shield. It moved Bum in front of it.

'What should I do?' Cindy cried. 'I can't get off a clear shot.'

Bum struggled. 'On the count of three I'm going to yank forward and down as hard as I can. Aim for the top of his head. The heat might startle him. He might let me go. Ready? One. Two . . .'

'Wait!' Cindy cried.

'What is it?' Bum asked.

'I've never shot someone before!'

'It's easy. Just pretend you're Sally.'

'I don't see how anyone can be Sally. How can I pretend to be her?'

Bum groaned as the creature bent back his arms. 'Then just close your eyes and pull the trigger when I get to three. I don't know how long I can hold out against this guy. Please Cindy.'

She nodded frantically. 'OK. Do it. Say it.'

'One. Two. Three!'

Bum yanked forward and ducked his head. Cindy took quick aim and fired. She did not shoot directly at the man's face, but just above his head. She could not bear to think of this man waking up with a burnt face if they somehow reversed the damage caused by the Cold People.

But Cindy's aim was not far off the creature's face. She singed its hair.

The creature let go of Bum, turned and fled.

He ran out the door howling.

Bum staggered to Cindy's side. He nodded as he took the flame thrower back. 'I'll tell Sally you wasted the guy,' he said.

Cindy smiled. 'Tell her there were ten of them.'

They loaded their equipment in the balloon. The fans and generator worked like a charm.

'What course?' Bum asked as they left the hardware store behind.

Cindy turned away from the direction of the lighthouse and her house. Like it or not, she realised all of Spooksville was her home. She had to help save it.

'Let's head for the hills,' she said. 'Let's help Adam and Sally.'

Twelve

Adam was feeling cold all over. Worse, he was having cold thoughts. As they roared out of town and into the hills, he kept looking over at Sally and thinking of all the warm blood in her veins. How he hated the fact that she was warm while he was cold.

How he wanted to make her cold too.

Adam knew the sick thoughts were from his wound.

He had to fight to keep the thoughts away.

He knew now he was slowly changing into a monster.

Sally glanced over at him. 'Are you OK?'

He nodded. 'Yeah. Just keep driving.'

'You don't look OK. How's your leg?'

'It's OK.'

'Can you feel it?' she asked.

'No.'

'Then how can you say it's OK?'

'Would you just shut up and drive!' Adam snapped. He stopped himself, dragging in a ragged breath. 'I'm sorry, Sally. I don't feel good. I feel cold. Could you please turn on the heater?'

'I have it all the way up. It's roasting in here. Has the numbing sensation spread?'

Adam smiled bitterly. 'Yeah. It's spreading.'

Spreading right into his brain.

He knew he did not have much time left.

The four-wheel drive was a wonderful machine. It allowed them not only to plough into the hills, but to keep going even when the road ran out. They blew past the reservoir at high speed. Just up ahead Adam could see the oil wells, bobbing up and down like giant insects. In the orange evening light, they looked ready to burn.

Soon the sun would set.

'Faster,' Adam whispered.

Finally they reached the oil wells. There were six of them, clustered round a series of eight storage tanks. Adam realised the lines from the wells fed the tanks, and that it was the tanks they had to crack. The suckers were huge. If they could drain them dry, there would be enough oil to fill the reservoir. The oil would just pour down into the water. He explained his thoughts to Sally.

But he did not tell her he could not stop thinking of how unfair it was that she was warm while he was shivering. He hoped the growing insanity did not show in his eyes.

'But we don't want to dynamite the tanks,' Sally said. 'They might catch fire. It's better the water goes into the reservoir.'

Adam sucked in another breath and tried to steady his shivering body. 'Take eight sticks of dynamite and cut off three quarters of each. Keep the fuses intact.' Adam had to struggle to get the words out. 'Plant a partial stick beneath each line that leads into each tank. If we blow all the lines, the oil will gush out.'

Sally watched him, worried. 'You sound weird. Your voice – you don't sound like Adam.'

He shook his head. 'I am still Adam. Just do it. Do it fast. We don't have much time.'

Sally reached out and touched his arm. But she withdrew her hand when she felt how cold he was. Her eyes were red; she was close to tears.

'Isn't there something I can do for you?' she begged.

Adam forced a smile. 'Save the world, Sally. That's all you can do.'

Sally took several dynamite sticks and walked to the storage tank lines. She carried a knife. Adam watched as she cut eight of the sticks down to a small size. Sally kept the flame thrower nearby.

She was planting them beneath the lines when Watch began to stir.

'Oh no,' Adam groaned. 'Just what we don't need.'

Watch sat up and looked at Adam.

In the evening gloom, his eyes glowed with evil light. Adam was too weak to flee.

'Watch,' Adam said gently. 'Don't do anything weird right now. We're almost home. Just sit here quietly and everything will be all right for all of us.'

Watch was not interested in his advice.

With one swift smash of his fist, Watch broke the glass that separated them. He reached over and grabbed Adam by the throat. Adam tried not to scream but he supposed he must have made some sound. He heard Sally scream and run towards them. Out of the corner of his eye he saw her raise the flame thrower. At the same time he felt Watch's cold breath on his cheek. He didn't know what his friend was going to do to him now but he imagined it was not going to be pleasant.

'Watch,' Adam gasped. 'You're my friend.'

The words had some effect. Watch hesitated for a

second. Like in the cemetery, the cold light in his eyes briefly faded. His blank expression contorted. It was like he was trying to remember Adam from another life. Perhaps he would have remembered him. But Sally arrived right then, and Sally did not believe in reasoning with a monster.

'Let him go!' Sally shouted as she aimed the flame thrower at the camper portion of the truck. 'Let him go or you're Liquid Drano!'

Watch released Adam and immediately turned on Sally. He did so by smashing through the side window of the camper and leaping outside. His speed was breathtaking. He stalked Sally but she kept him at a distance with her flame thrower. Yet she was not willing to burn him, and Watch seemed to know that now. He did not seem as frightened of the fire as before.

And Sally had other problems.

Her flame seemed to shorten even as she pulled harder on the trigger.

'I'm running out of fuel!' she called anxiously to Adam.

'Back up in the direction of the dynamite sticks!' Adam shouted. 'We must blow those lines and we must blow them now!'

'We still have to light the oil once it's in the

reservoir!' Sally called. She listened to his direction, however. Keeping an eye and the flame on Watch, she managed to steer herself back to the tanks. There she broke into a jog, brushing each stick's fuse with her flame as she passed. It was a dangerous manoeuvre. If her aim was only slightly off, the dynamite would go off in her face.

But Sally had a steady hand: soon all the fuses were burning bright.

However, Sally's flame thrower continued to fail. She tried getting back to Adam and the truck but at each turn Watch blocked her way. Watch seemed particularly intent on getting to her. Perhaps he remembered how she had knocked him over the head in the cemetery.

'I can't reach you!' Sally cried.

'It doesn't matter,' Adam called back. 'Just get away from the oil lines.'

Sally did as he told her, even as Watch continued to stalk her. 'I can't hold him off much longer!'

'Listen,' Adam called. 'Just as the sticks explode, make a dash down the hill. I'll slip the truck into neutral. I'll pick you up as I coast by.'

'But your leg is numb!' Sally shouted back. 'You won't be able to brake!'

'I'll do the best I can,' Adam said.

Ten seconds later the sticks began to explode. They went in a tight series, one after the other. The explosions seemed to check Watch. He froze – of course, he was already frozen – and Sally had a chance to run down the hill towards the reservoir. She just dropped the flame thrower and split.

She was not the only thing that raced towards the reservoir.

As the last dynamite stick went off, Adam saw a large wave of oil chasing Sally. The line to each tank had ruptured. It was a black tidal wave. No question about it – the reservoir would be flooded with fuel.

Adam dragged himself into driver's seat and released the handbrake. The truck began to coast down the hill, rapidly picking up speed. He was able to steer, but by now both his legs were without feeling. Sally was right – he could not brake. By the time he reached her he was doing fifty kilometres an hour. There was no way she could even leap on to the truck.

'Adam!' she yelled.

'Sorry!' he shouted back as he flew past.

Adam was able to keep from plunging into the water by turning sharply to the right just as he reached the bottom of the hill. His wild steering sent up a huge dust cloud. The sharp turn also took him out of the way of the approaching oil wave. Unfortunately, he had also put more distance between himself and Sally. Distance he could not make up by driving over and picking her up. His legs refused to work. He could turn on the engine but he could not put the car in gear.

He was stuck where he was.

He saw Sally reach the water just before Watch. But she had no flame thrower to ward him off. She didn't even have a good stick. Desperately looking in his direction, Adam could see the fear in her eyes even though she was at least a hundred metres away.

'What should I do?' she screamed.

There was only one hope.

'Jump in the water!' Adam yelled. 'Swim out to the middle of the reservoir!'

'But this water's poisonous! It makes your hair all funny!'

'Don't worry about that now! He's coming right towards you!'

Sally could see that she didn't have many options. Watch was now only ten metres away and closing. Whirling, Sally dashed into the reservoir and began to swim frantically away from the shore. For a moment it seemed Watch would try to follow her. But like the creatures that fell into the witch's moat, he seemed uneasy about the water. Plus, he could not stay where he was. The oil was close on his heels. Watch was forced to run to the side.

Luckily for Adam, he ran to the other side.

Now Adam had a wave of oil between him and Watch.

He had to make the toughest decision of his life.

The oil was flooding the reservoir at an incredible rate. In just a few minutes he should be able to ignite the slick with the box of dynamite he still had beside him. The only trouble was Sally had to stay in the water to stay away from Watch, and if she did stay there she would burn. Sally could not even circle round to reach Adam. The oil slick had already come between the two of them. Sally could only swim towards the centre of the reservoir.

Adam could not kill her. He knew this.

But he could not let all of Spooksville die either.

He knew that as well.

He pulled the case of dynamite with him as he crawled out of the truck.

He had Sally's Bic lighter. He just had to set the case next to the shore. The oil would reach him soon. Then he had to set the fuse, light it and crawl away. He could make the fuse as long as he liked. He could give Sally as many extra minutes as she asked for. The trouble was none of those minutes would be enough. Even if she could out-swim the growing slick, and reach the other side, Watch would be waiting for her.

Adam could not believe how horrible the situation was.

And he was so cold. He could not stop shaking.

But he had hit rock bottom before.

He should have known that when things were at their worst, they often got better.

From out of nowhere Adam saw a balloon in the sky. Not just any balloon, but one carrying Cindy and Bum. His friends seemed to understand the dilemma. For they were heading straight towards Sally, swooping down out of the orange evening sky. Their balloon was powered by what looked like hardware store fans. They had speed and steering ability.

Sally saw them and waved her arms frantically.

The oil slick was closing on her.

Adam broke open the case of dynamite and pulled out his longest fuse.

The oil slick was moving his way as well.

The balloon dipped low. Cindy reached over the edge.

Adam set his fuse and grabbed the lighter.

Sally reached up and grabbed Cindy's hand.

The oil slick touched Sally's foot just as she was pulled into the balloon.

The slick touched crippled Adam just as he lit the fuse and began to crawl away from the water. Far across the black reservoir, Watch seemed to finally understand what they were trying to do. He let out a high pitched howl.

But there was nothing he could do to stop them.

The balloon rose high into the sky.

Adam crawled clear of the oil.

The dynamite exploded. The reservoir caught fire.

It lit up the sky. It lit up the heavens.

The temperature began to climb. In the hills and in the city.

All over Spooksville, the original Cryo creatures began to melt.

And those they had changed returned to normal.

Even Adam. The feeling returned to his whole body.

Even Watch, who had not been normal to begin with.

Epilogue

When it was all over, and the fire had finally begun to die down, the friends drove the four-wheel truck back to town. This time Bum drove. He didn't have a licence either, but he seemed familiar with gear shifts. Cindy sat up front with Bum. Adam and Sally were in the back with Watch.

The last thing Watch remembered was thawing out the block of ice.

He didn't even remember the cold man.

But he believed everything they told him. And he seemed unmoved by the fact he had almost killed all of them. Sally frowned at his lack of feelings on the matter.

'I think you're still a little cold,' she said.

'I always have been,' Watch agreed. 'But what I still want to know is why these creatures showed up now? Who put them here?'

'I think that's a riddle for another day,' Bum said from the front.

'I hope I never live to see the day those things return,' Cindy said.

'Hey, let's look on the bright side,' Adam said. 'We had another incredible adventure and we came out winners. We should celebrate.'

'Yeah,' Watch said. 'Let's go get some ice-cream.'

A silence fell over the truck.

None of them thought that was a good idea.

Spooksville 6

THE WITCH'S REVENGE

One

The argument was old. Was Ms Ann Templeton, Spooksville's most powerful and beautiful resident, a good witch or a bad witch? There was no question whether she was a *real* witch. Adam and his friends had seen too many demonstrations of her power to doubt that. But whereas Adam and Watch liked to think she was a nice person, Sally and Cindy were certain she was dangerous.

The argument started in the Frozen Cow, Spooksville's best known ice-cream parlour. The owner would only serve vanilla, so they were all having vanilla shakes when the idea of visiting the witch's castle came up. Of course, later, they would blame each other for the idea. Later, that is, when they couldn't find their way out of the castle.

It was a hot summer Wednesday, ten o'clock in the

1

morning, a perfect time for a milk shake. School was still a few weeks away. As was often the case, they were trying to decide what they were going to do with the day.

'We can't go to the beach because of the sharks,' Sally said as she listed the various possibilities. 'We can't go to the lighthouse because we burned that down. We can't go to the reservoir because we burned that up as well. And we can't go to the Haunted Cave because it's haunted.' She paused. 'Maybe we should try to contact Eckweel and go for another ride on a flying saucer.'

Watch shook his head. 'We forgot to get a communication device from him. We have no way to contact him.'

But he promised to call us some day,' Adam said.

'Yes,' Sally replied. 'But he's an alien. They have a different perspective on time. Some day might be ten thousand years from now for him.'

'I thought you didn't like Eckweel,' Cindy said to Sally. 'You kept calling him Fat Head.'

'I called him that because he had a fat head,' Sally said. 'That does not mean I disliked him. I call you plenty of names and I still like you. Most of the time.' Sally added.

Cindy was not impressed. 'I am *so* relieved.'

'What if we didn't do anything special today?' Adam suggested. 'What if we just hung out and relaxed? We could play checkers or chess or something.'

Sally stared at him as if he had lost his mind. 'Are you all right, Adam?'

'I'm fine,' he said. 'Just because I want to have a relaxing day doesn't mean there's anything wrong with me.'

'But this is Spooksville,' Sally said. 'We don't relax here. That's the first thing that will get you killed. You always have to be on your guard.'

'I don't see how playing chess could be dangerous,' Adam said. 'Even in Spooksville.'

'Ha,' Sally said, turning to Watch. 'Tell him what happened to Sandy Stone.'

Watch frowned. 'We're not sure if the game did it to her.'

'Of course we are,' Sally said. 'She was playing on the witch's chess board when it happened.'

'What happened to her?' Cindy asked.

Sally shrugged. 'She turned to stone. What would you expect with a name like Sandy Stone?'

'Is that true?' Adam asked Watch.

Watch appeared uncertain. 'Well, we did find a

3

stone statue of Sandy not far from the witch's castle. And the statue was sitting in front of a mysterious looking chess board.'

'I don't understand,' Cindy said.

'Chess was Sandy's favourite game,' Sally explained. 'She was a master of it. She could beat anyone in the city. The trouble is, she boasted about the fact, and apparently Ms Witch Ann Templeton heard about it, and didn't like it. The witch plays chess herself, and sent out a challenge to Sandy, which Sandy accepted.' Sally paused and shook her head. 'And that was the last time any of us saw her alive.'

'Are you saying the witch turned her to stone because Sandy lost to her?' Adam asked.

'It may have been because Sandy beat the witch,' Sally said. 'The witch is a well-known bad loser.'

'Is the stone statue still there?' Cindy asked.

'No,' Watch said. 'It was made of soft stone, like compressed sand. After the first good storm it was gone. Down the gutter.'

Cindy glanced at Adam. 'Do you believe this?' she asked.

Adam shrugged. 'Ms Ann Templeton never seemed that bad to me.'

Sally snorted. 'Just because she's pretty and she

smiled at you, Adam, you're willing to forgive a dozen years of murder and genocide.'

'What does genocide mean?' Adam asked Watch.

'Unpleasant behaviour towards many people,' Watch said uncertainly.

'I can't believe she would murder anyone,' Adam said.

Sally threw her head back and laughed. 'You are too much! What about those friendly bodyguards of hers we met while we were in the Haunted Cave? Have you forgotten how they tried to spear us for dinner? Do you think they were just playing? Do you think she didn't approve of their hunting habits?'

'But it was Ann Templeton who gave Bum and me the clues for how to find you guys while you were trapped in the cave,' Watch said.

'Yeah,' Adam said. 'She also gave Watch the magic words that helped us rescue the Hyeet from the Haunted Cave. How do you explain that?'

Sally replied with exaggerated patience. 'She told Watch how to get into the cave because she thought there was no way he would get out. She probably told him the magic word because she was hoping we would all get trapped in another dimension.'

'But when the Cold People attacked,' Adam said,

'she was one of the few people who really tried to fight them off.'

'She was trying to save her own skin,' Sally said. 'Nothing else.'

'For once I have to agree with Sally,' Cindy said reluctantly. 'I saw those trolls she keeps in her basement. She must be an evil witch to have such monsters in her castle.'

'Not necessarily,' Adam said. 'She might just feel sorry for them. I would imagine trolls have trouble finding places to live.'

Sally stared at him. 'I can't believe you just said that. Her castle may be many dark things but it is not a refuge for homeless trolls.'

'I have never actually seen her hurt someone with my own eyes,' Watch said.

'Yeah, but you're half blind,' Sally said. 'You have never actually seen the sun come up.'

'I can see the sun,' Watch said quietly, perhaps hurt by the remark. 'I can see the moon, too, as long as I have my glasses on.'

'A lot of these stories about people dying and disappearing might have nothing to do with her,' Adam said. 'They might be caused by natural creatures, like aliens and ghosts and things.'

'But if she isn't evil,' Cindy said to Adam, 'why is everyone so afraid of her?'

Adam shrugged. 'People believe all kinds of nasty rumours.' He added, 'You know, she invited me to her castle once.'

'But even you were not stupid enough to accept her invitation,' Sally said. 'Which just proves my point. Deep inside you know she would just as soon eat your heart out as smile at you.'

'That's not true,' Adam said. 'The only reason I haven't visited her at her castle is because I've been too busy since I moved here.'

'You're not busy today,' Sally mocked.

'I wouldn't mind visiting her at her castle,' Watch said softly, almost to himself. 'I have heard she has the power to heal. I wonder if she could do something about my eyes.'

To everyone's surprise, Sally reached over and squeezed Watch's hand. 'Your eyes are fine the way they are,' she said. 'You don't need to be healed by that witch. I shouldn't have said what I did about your vision. I'm sorry, Watch.'

Cindy glanced at Adam. 'I can't believe she just apologised,' she said.

'I've seen her do it once before,' Adam said.

Sally spoke seriously to all of them. 'No one's going to the castle. There're alligators and crocodiles in her moat that would eat you alive before you could even get inside. Believe me, the place is a death trap.'

'But there's a drawbridge,' Watch said. 'If she wants us to enter, she'll let it down.'

Adam studied Watch. 'You really do want to go, don't you? Do your eyes bother you that much?'

Watch looked away, out of the window of the ice-cream parlour. 'Well, you know, I don't like to complain.'

'Complain,' Adam said. 'You're with friends. How are your eyes?'

'I don't know,' Watch said. Briefly he removed his glasses and cleaned them on his shirt. When he put them back on, he squinted into the distance. 'I think they're getting worse.'

Cindy was concerned. 'Can't you get stronger glasses?'

Watch spoke reluctantly. Clearly the subject embarrassed him. 'The doctors say no. You see, it's not just a focusing problem. Everything seems to be getting dimmer, like it's always evening-time.'

'How is it at night-time?' Adam asked.

'I can't really see then at all,' Watch said. 'Not any more. I just bump into things.'

Sally was worried. 'You never told us.'

Watch shook his head. 'There's nothing you guys can do.'

'But you should have told Eckweel,' Cindy said. 'Remember the way he fixed my ankle with his healing machine?'

'They weren't as bad then,' Watch said. 'And I didn't want to bother him.'

'Watch,' Adam said, frustrated. 'He's our friend. He would have been happy to help you.'

Watch lowered his head. 'Well, he's gone now. And we don't know when he'll be coming back.'

'But maybe Ann Templeton can help you,' Adam said. 'I think it's worth the risk to ask her. Why don't we do that now?'

'Do what?' Cindy asked.

'Go to the castle,' Adam said simply.

Sally and Cindy looked at each other. 'The boys have lost their minds,' Sally said.

'They're looking for help in all the wrong places,' Cindy agreed.

'You two don't have to come,' Adam said. 'If you're scared.'

'I'm not scared,' Sally said. 'I am just a reasonable, thinking, human being. Calling on evil witches – even

9

in the middle of the day – is just plain stupid. She won't heal Watch's eyes. More likely, she'll carve them out with one of her long red nails and have them in her evening soup.'

'She wouldn't have such a terrible reputation if she hadn't done something bad,' Cindy added.

'I trust my own instincts,' Adam said. 'I think she's a good witch. What do you say, Watch?'

Watch nodded enthusiastically. 'I want to visit her. I think she'll welcome us, especially since she's already invited you.'

'This is going to be a long day,' Sally said darkly.

Two

The walk to Ann Templeton's castle was not long. The group had been near the place before, of course, while fighting the Cold People. The castle was located on a hill overlooking the cemetery. From its front porch one could see the ocean as well. As they approached, Adam imagined that Ann Templeton had a wonderful view up and down the coast from the top of her highest tower.

From the outside, it appeared a medium-sized castle, but Adam knew from experience that its basements ran deep. Made of mostly large grey blocks of stone, it was surrounded by a wide moat that at first glance looked like a pleasant pond. But if one stared long enough, large dark shapes could be seen moving beneath the water.

There was no doorknob or bell on the outer wall.

Adam wondered how they were supposed to make their presence known. He said as much to the others but Sally thought that was the least of their concerns.

'She knows we're here,' Sally said. 'No one gets near her place without her knowing.'

Cindy gestured to the moat. 'Has anybody ever fallen in there?'

'I have heard she pushed a few kids in the moat from the top of her tower,' Sally said. 'You could hear their screams miles away.'

Cindy turned to Adam. 'I still think this is a bad idea,' she said.

Adam was getting annoyed at the girls' gloomy outlook. 'We told you that you and Sally should stay at home.'

'Yeah, but you accused us of being cowards,' Sally said. 'So in a sense you forced us to come.'

Cindy jumped suddenly. 'What's that?'

That was the sound of the drawbridge slowly lowering. The group all backed up. The wide wooden plank creaked as it descended; the metal gears sounded as if they hadn't been used in ages. Adam wondered if Ann Templeton had another route for leaving the castle.

The drawbridge came to a dust-shaking halt a few

metres in front of them. It was made of thick boards. Obviously it could support their weight. Yet as the drawbridge settled, they noticed that the crocodiles and the alligators came closer to the surface. Adam saw several pairs of hungry eyes peering at him.

'She might try to raise it the second we step on it,' Sally warned.

'We would slide straight into the water,' Cindy agreed.

'I think she's welcoming us,' Adam said, stepping on to the edge of the drawbridge. 'I think it would be rude to ignore her welcome.'

'Better to be rude than to be dead,' Sally said.

Watch stepped all the way on to the bridge. 'I don't care about the rest of you. I'm going to go talk to her.'

Adam stopped him. 'Before we go inside, I want you to know there's probably only a small chance she can help with your eyes. I mean, I just don't want you to get your hopes up.'

Watch smiled faintly. 'I know that, Adam. You don't have to worry about me. I always get by.'

Sally looked at Cindy. 'Stop them.'

'How am I supposed to stop them?' Cindy asked.

'I don't know,' Sally said. 'You always get Adam to do what you want.'

'Adam, don't go inside,' Cindy said. 'Please.'

'I have to go,' Adam said. He tugged on Watch's arm. 'Come on, we'll go alone. There's no reason for the girls to risk it.'

Cindy turned to Sally. 'That didn't work.'

Sally came alongside Adam. 'No reason for the girls to risk it? There you go again, another sexist statement. Cindy and I can take whatever risks you guys are taking.'

'I wish you wouldn't drag me into your feminist philosophy,' Cindy said, even though she also hurried to catch up with them.

The front door was huge. Had the four of them stood on each other's shoulders, they would have been unable to reach the top of it. There was no doorbell but instead there was a huge gold skull-shaped door-knocker. Sally did not like the design of the knocker.

'When have you ever seen a skull on the door of a good witch?' she said.

'It's decorative,' Adam said as he reached up to use it. He knocked gently a couple of times, and then took a step back. He did not know what sort of creature would answer the door, or if it would be Ann Templeton herself. But he was sure somebody would answer. That was why he was so surprised when the door slowly began to swing open all by itself. As a group, they stared into the vast dark interior. They could see a fire place burning in a grate in the distance, but little else.

'Hello!' Adam called.

His voice echoed as it trailed off into the distance.

No one called back.

'Could the castle be empty?' Cindy wondered aloud.

'If it's empty, then who opened the door?' Watch said.

'It could be a magic door,' Sally said.

'I don't think the place is empty,' Adam said. 'You don't just go and leave a castle without someone to guard it.' He gestured to the open door. 'I think we're being invited inside.'

'Why isn't she here to make the invitation in person?' Sally said. 'This feels like a set-up to me. As soon as we step inside, the door will close at our backs. Then the trolls will come, and then we'll be dead meat.'

Adam stuck his head through the open door. Beside the distant fireplace, he could see a row of burning torches lighting a long hallway. But the actual walls of the room, the furniture it may have held, were hidden in the shadows.

'I don't see any trolls,' Adam muttered.

'You don't see a butler in a tuxedo either,' Sally said. 'This is too weird. I say we turn around now, have another vanilla shake at the Frozen Cow, and consider ourselves lucky we listened to me.'

Watch stepped forward. 'I've been in darker places. I don't mind doing a little exploring.'

Adam followed him. 'If she wants to hurt us, she could have hurt us already.'

Sally chased after them. 'If she wants to hurt you, you don't have to make it easy for her.'

Cindy also followed them inside. 'We don't even have a flashlight,' she fretted.

They were barely inside when the door slammed shut at their backs.

The noise made them jump.

'I'm not going to say I told you so,' Sally whispered in the dark. 'But I did.'

Three

The entrance room was vast; it also seemed to be made largely of grey stone. As their eyes adjusted to the dim light cast by the fireplace and the torches in the nearby hall, Adam saw that the place was empty. There was no furniture, no ornaments or paintings of any kind. He wondered if Ann Templeton ever came into this room. Although it was free of dust and other signs of age, it felt as if it had been deserted for a long time.

'It's cold in here,' Cindy said, shivering.

'It is a psychic chill you feel,' Sally said. 'Your soul realises it has entered a place of great evil, from which there is no escape.'

'I kind of like this place,' Watch said, squinting in the dark.

'It's good to be out of the sun,' Adam agreed.

'You guys are in a state of denial,' Sally snapped.

'We're already in danger and you refuse to admit it. Where is Ms Ann Templeton? She knows we're here. The only reason she hasn't appeared is because she is playing some weird game with us. And her games are always dangerous.'

'I wouldn't mind leaving now,' Cindy said, glancing nervously round.

'I want to see what's at the end of this hallway,' Adam said, gesturing to the torch-lit passageway. He and Watch stepped into the narrow stone hallway. The girls followed a few steps behind, whispering to themselves about how stupid boys were.

'Can you see where you're going?' Adam asked Watch.

'I'm OK,' his friend said. 'Do you think she's here?'

'She must be here,' Adam said.

'I hope we meet her before we run into one of her trolls,' said Watch.

'I think she keeps them in the basement,' Adam replied.

'I wonder what else she keeps there,' Watch said.

The hallway was long. It wound left and right. Finally they entered another large room. This one was also lit by torches and a single massive fireplace, but it was decorated like an ancient castle chamber should be, with over-sized gold-framed furniture, and giant paintings of forgotten battles. There was even a throne inlaid with gems at the far end of the room. But that was not what caught their eyes.

In the centre of the chamber was a huge hourglass.

In place of sand fell sparkling jewel dust.

The dust glowed like stars, as it dropped, counting the seconds.

'We've seen this before,' Adam said, touching the hourglass. It was twice their height, and was supported with a shiny stand made of gold and silver.

'Where?' Cindy asked.

'On the other side of the Secret Path,' Sally said. 'In the evil witch's castle. We didn't tell you about her, but she was a real pain. Except on the other side of the Secret Path the sand flowed upwards – probably because time flowed backwards in that dimension.' Sally paused. 'In fact, the evil witch said that Ann Templeton had a similar hourglass. It was as if she wanted us to know. Do you guys remember?'

'I do,' Watch said. 'I also remember that her evil sister's hourglass was the main source of her power.'

Sally rested her palm on the hourglass, her face lit with colour from the sparkling dust. 'I wonder if this is the source of Ann Templeton's power,' she said, a

19

mischievous note in her voice. 'If we hold it all in our hands.'

'I think you two are forgetting something,' Adam said. 'When we broke the other hourglass, the whole place went crazy. Everything started to fall apart. We have to be careful with this hourglass. Who knows what would happen to our world if we damaged it?'

'I wasn't thinking of breaking it,' Sally said.

'We believe you,' Watch said.

'It's incredibly beautiful,' Cindy said. 'I wonder what this sand is made of. It looks like stardust.'

'It might be *real* stardust,' Watch said. 'It definitely has some kind of power.'

'But that brings me back to my original questions,' Sally said. 'Why does she let us find these things? Why isn't she here to explain what we're looking at? I still think this is some kind of set-up. We have to be careful.'

Adam pointed to another narrow hallway. 'Let's check down there.'

'If we take hallway after hallway,' Cindy warned, 'we'll end up lost.'

'She has a point,' Sally said. 'You notice we haven't really gone underground, and yet we've already covered a lot of ground, more ground than the castle seems to cover from the outside.'

'What are you saying?' Adam asked.

Sally spoke seriously. 'We might be in another dimension already, and not know it.'

'I think you're jumping to your usual grim conclusions,' Watch said.

'We'll see,' Sally said.

They walked down the next hallway, and soon came to another room. This one was not as large as the previous one, nor were there as many decorations or furniture. But there were another two blazing fireplaces. With all the fires, Adam wondered that the castle was not shrouded in smoke on the outside. Yet in spite of the fires, the room was as cold as the others.

In the centre of the chamber were four necklaces.

They rested on a white sheet. Each held a different coloured precious stone: a green emerald, a red ruby, a blue sapphire, a yellow topaz. The jewels were exquisite, perfectly polished, and large – Adam decided they must be worth a fortune. They were each attached to a fine gold band. The gold also wrapped around each stone, like a miniature claw, and held the gem in place. In front of each necklace was a small card with a single printed word on it.

21

Before the emerald was the word IMMORTALITY.

Beside the ruby was the word STRENGTH.

In front of the sapphire was the word MATURITY.

Next to the yellow topaz the card said BEAUTY.

The stones seemed to shimmer with a light of their own making. As the four of them approached, they found they could not stop staring at the stones. Adam in particular was drawn to the blue sapphire. He didn't know why, but he felt as if Ann Templeton had laid it out specially for him. Being on the short side for his age, he had always wanted to be older, more mature. He had no doubt that each stone was capable of giving the quality listed beside it. For some reason, he immediately assumed they were magical necklaces.

Adam went to touch the sapphire when Sally stopped him.

'Don't,' she said. 'It's a trap.'

Adam had to blink to clear his head. He realised, in a space of a few seconds, that the stones had almost hypnotised him. 'What are you talking about?' he asked.

'She wants us to put these on,' Sally said.

'I don't want to put one of them on,' Cindy said.

Sally eyed her suspiciously. 'Aren't you attracted to one of them, Cindy?'

Cindy seemed embarrassed. 'Well, the yellow topaz looks nice.'

'Which one do you like, Watch?' Sally asked.

'The red ruby,' Watch said.

'Adam?' Sally said.

'I like the blue one,' Adam said. 'But so what?'

'I like the green emerald,' Sally said. 'I was immediately drawn to it. Like you, I went to reach out and put it on. But then I remembered where we are, who we're dealing with.' She paused. 'The necklaces have been placed here to tempt each of us. They're designed to do that.'

'I still don't know what you're talking about,' Cindy said.

'The witch knows us,' Sally said. 'She can probably read our minds. For example, she knows that you, Cindy, are obsessed with your appearance.'

Cindy was insulted. 'That's ridiculous! I'm not vain.'

'You're as vain as a Persian cat,' Sally said. 'You're not attracted to the topaz because you like the stone. You like the idea of what it can do for you. Listen, I'm not singling you out. You guys are always talking about how I am obsessed with death. Well, what I'm really interested in is living forever.'

'Sally might have a point,' Adam said. 'I'm drawn to the sapphire, and I think it's because it can make me older and wiser.'

Cindy shook her head. 'It never occurred to me to want to look more beautiful.'

'Fine,' Sally said. 'Then there's no need for you to try the topaz necklace on.'

'I can try it on if I want,' Cindy said.

Sally snorted. 'I bet you put it on the second I look away.'

'You could be right,' Watch said. 'I am drawn to the ruby. I think if it gives me strength, it will probably make my eyes and ears stronger as well. I want to try it on. I think I'm going to in a second, just to see if it does work.'

Sally was exasperated. 'Are you crazy? You think we will get these qualities for free? The witch will make us pay for whatever these stones can do for us.'

'How do we know they can do anything for us?' Cindy interrupted. 'They might just be pretty pieces of jewellery.'

'Because we're in a witch's castle,' Sally said. 'Not a shopping mall. The witch has got magic, I never said she didn't. But it's black magic. I say we get out of here now.'

'As you've said before,' Adam muttered.

24

'Good advice cannot be repeated too often,' Sally said.

'But if we leave now,' Watch warned, 'we'll never know what these necklaces might have done for us.' He reached for the ruby. 'I'll try this. Just me. The rest of you can see if anything happens to me.'

Sally quickly grabbed his arm. 'No! What if you turn into a frog?'

'I have never seen a strong frog,' Cindy remarked.

'Maybe she does want to trick us,' Watch said to Sally, who continued to hold on to his arm. 'But maybe she wants to help us. We've had this argument already. The only way we can know is for one of us to put on one of these necklaces.' He reached down and gently removed Sally's fingers. 'Don't worry, if I turn into something gross you can always put me in the creek. I sort of like the place.'

Sally shook her head and took a step back. 'It's your life.'

'And I'm not getting any younger,' Watch agreed.

He reached down and put the ruby necklace over his head.

He paused and looked round, blinking several times.

The rest of them held their breath.

'Interesting,' Watch finally muttered.

'Do you feel strong?' Adam asked.

Watch flexed his arms, squeezed his fingers.

'I feel slightly different,' he said.

'But do you feel stronger?' Sally demanded.

Watch continued to flex his muscles, to look around. 'Yes. I feel just a tiny bit stronger. And I think I can see slightly better.'

'You might just be imagining the changes,' Cindy warned.

Watch stretched out his arms and took a few steps around the room. 'I don't think so. I could barely see this room at all a few seconds ago. Now I can see the walls, the details on the brick-work.' He paused. 'The effect is growing as time passes. Already I can see better than when I first put on the necklace.'

Adam laughed nervously. 'If you keep getting stronger so fast, soon your muscles will bulge out of your clothes.'

Watch smiled, which he rarely did. He fingered the necklace lovingly. 'I like this thing. I think you guys should try on the other ones.'

Cindy reached for the topaz. 'All right. But I can't imagine that I could look any more beautiful than I already do.'

Sally grabbed her arm. 'Wait a second! This has been no experiment. We have to observe Watch for a while, see how he changes.'

Cindy shook her off. 'But we can see already that the change is for the better. If I want to try on the necklace, I can. You're not the boss, you know.'

'I should be,' Sally said.

'Maybe I should be the next one to try a necklace,' Adam said, staring at the sapphire again. 'Let us guys take the risks.'

'Ha,' Cindy said. 'Let you guys get to enjoy all the magic is what you mean. Let's try on the necklaces together. That's fair.'

Sally continued to shake her head. 'You're all going to turn into toads. I'm going to have to go down to the creek every day just to see you guys.'

Adam and Cindy ignored her. Together they put on the necklace they were most drawn to. Adam liked the feel of it as it went over his neck. He stroked the sapphire as it hung close to his heart. He glanced over at Cindy who beamed back at him.

'How do I look?' she asked.

'The same,' Sally muttered. 'Like a stick-in-the-mud.'

'No,' Watch said, stepping closer to Cindy. 'I think you look better. Adam?'

Adam studied Cindy. 'Yeah. She looks more radiant. Like she's glowing.'

Cindy grinned and rubbed her bare arms. 'I feel more beautiful. I feel – it's hard to describe – like I'm filling up with light.'

'I feel like I'm getting a headache,' Sally moaned. 'How about you, Adam? Are you older and wiser?'

Adam frowned. 'It's like Cindy said. It's hard to describe. I feel some kind of change – a little stronger, a little smarter maybe.'

'I think you look a little taller,' Watch said.

'Yeah, he's definitely not as short,' Cindy said enthusiastically.

Adam was taken back. 'I didn't know you thought I was short to begin with.'

Cindy patted his shoulder. 'I didn't mean you were short-short. You just weren't . . . as tall as Watch.' She paused and burst out laughing. 'But what does it matter now? You're going to be taller than all of us. Hey, Sally, go ahead, put on your necklace.'

'Yeah,' Adam said. 'If it does work, and it makes you immortal, then nothing's going to hurt you anyway. What do you have to lose?'

Sally glanced at the emerald necklace. 'Are you sure you guys feel better?'

Cindy began to dance about the room. 'I feel like a beautiful princess. I *am* a princess!'

'I can definitely see better,' Watch said, taking off his glasses.

'And I definitely feel less like a kid,' Adam said.

Sally reached out and touched the necklace, but then withdrew her hand. 'But don't you like feeling like a kid?' she said.

'I think these necklaces are gifts,' Adam said simply.

'I guess I'll have to trust you guys,' Sally said.

And with that she reached down and lifted the emerald necklace and placed it over her head. For a moment she stood fingering the beautiful green stone. Then she looked up and let out a laugh.

'Now I feel more like a kid,' she exclaimed.

Another wave of laughter sounded. But it did not come from any of them. This laughter was older, deeper and darker, and maybe a little wicked. It came from the direction of yet another hallway, that none of them had noticed at first because it had been unlit. But now a tall figure in a black cloak was walking their way, clasping a burning torch in her hand. Her green eyes glimmered in the stone passageway, even before she entered the room, and Adam was reminded of the emerald in Sally's magical necklace. For right then

Adam was convinced they were in the presence of great magic. But whether it was white or black, he was not yet sure.

'It's the witch,' Sally whispered, scared.

'Shh,' Adam warned. 'Don't call her that.'

'But I don't mind,' Ann Templeton said as she stepped into the room and threw back the cape on her cloak. She smiled as she said it, even laughed, but in her green eyes was a light more dangerous than any light they had ever seen before. Cold as the glow of a frosty dawn, but as powerful as the light of a distant star. She added, 'I'm your favourite witch.'

Four

'What do you want?' Sally asked suspiciously. Instinctively, they had all gathered together. Cindy was, in fact, holding on to Adam's arm. They even backed up a step as Ann Templeton came further into the room. She was like Adam remembered, beautiful with her long dark hair and her piercing green eyes. She was also as pale as he recalled; it did not seem like she often saw the sun. She smiled slyly at Sally's question, as she stood tall and in command in front of them.

'Shouldn't I be the one to ask that question?' she said. 'You four are the ones, after all, who came here looking for something.'

'We don't want anything from you,' Sally snapped.

Ann Templeton was amused. 'Oh, Sara. Then why have you tried to steal my necklaces?'

Adam stuttered. 'We didn't intend to steal anything, ma'am. We just wanted to try them on. We can put them back now if you want.'

Ann Templeton continued to wear a smile. 'Do you think you can just put them back, Adam?' she asked. 'Do you think it's that simple?'

'I'll put mine back if you don't want me to have it,' Watch said. He took hold of the necklace and began to pull it back over his head. 'We thought maybe they were gifts, but we're sorry if we made a mistake.'

Then Watch froze, the necklace half way over his head.

He looked stunned with surprise.

'What is it?' Sally asked nervously.

'I can't get it off,' Watch said.

'What do you mean you can't get it off?' Sally asked. 'Just take it off.'

'You try taking yours off,' Watch said.

Sally reached down and started to pull the necklace over her head. But she could only get halfway there. The fine gold band that carried the stone refused to pass all the way over her head.

'Oh no,' Sally whispered.

Adam and Cindy tried to take off their necklaces.

But they couldn't get them over their heads.

Ann Templeton laughed softly to herself.

'Do you still think it's that simple?' she asked.

Sally took a step forward. 'You tricked us.'

Ann Templeton shook her head. 'No. You tricked yourselves. I didn't make you put on the necklaces. If you had come here not wanting anything, you wouldn't be in this situation right now.'

'Are we in trouble?' Adam asked. 'I mean, I kind of like this necklace. If it's stuck around my head, I don't mind.' Then he added, 'As long as you don't mind that I keep it?'

Ann Templeton stared at him. 'That is sweet of you to say so, Adam. Actually, I made these necklaces for each of you. Certainly you may keep them. If you meet just one condition.'

'What is that?' Sally asked suspiciously.

'My condition is simple,' Ann Templeton said. 'You just have to find your way out of my castle. If you do, then you may keep your necklace. You can even take it off and put it back on whenever you wish.' She added in a more menacing tone, 'But as long as you're in my castle, you can't take off the necklace. No matter how hard you try.'

'But we know how to get out of here,' Watch said. 'We just have to walk back to the hourglass room, and then through the hallway on the right, and then we'll come back to the front door.'

'Where is the hourglass room?' Ann Templeton asked in a slightly mocking tone.

'It's just over . . .' Watch began, before his voice trailed into silence.

The hallway through which they had entered was gone.

'Am I confused?' Watch asked Adam.

Adam shook his head. 'No. The hallway's vanished.'

'It disappeared the moment all four of you had put on your necklaces,' said Ann Templeton.

'It's just as I thought,' Sally said bitterly. 'This has all been a set-up to trap us. I told you guys she was an evil witch.'

Sally's outburst caused Ann Templeton to laugh heartily. 'The necklaces are not here to trap you, Sara. They're here to test you.'

'How?' Watch asked.

'You will see,' Ann Templeton said as she turned to leave. 'Now I have to get back to my own affairs. I will give you only one piece of advice while you stumble around trying to find your way out of here.' She paused. 'Watch out for my boys.'

Cindy gulped. 'Who are your boys?'

Ann Templeton. 'My boys are like boys everywhere. Full of fun and mischief. But their idea of fun might not be the same as your idea of fun.' She laughed at that. 'Try to stay out of their way!'

With that Ann Templeton strode back up the hallway from which she had emerged. As her torch began to fade in the long darkness, they noticed that the opening to the hallway had vanished – leaving them trapped in a room that seemed to have no way out.

Five

'Now what are we going to do?' Sally grumbled.

'She said this is a test,' Adam said. 'That means there must be a way out of this room. What do you say, Watch?'

Watch continued to flex his arms and hands. 'I hope that's true. But if it's not, it won't matter anyway if I keep growing stronger like this. I'll be able to tear down these walls.'

Adam nodded as he studied his own body. The floor definitely looked further away. 'I'm changing fast as well,' he said. 'I think I must be thirteen years old by now.'

Sally, who looked an inch shorter, made a sarcastic swooning sound. 'Oh, an older man. How exciting.'

'I'm not ready to panic yet.' Cindy said. 'I'm still

excited about my necklace.' She paused. 'I wish I had a mirror. Do I look as pretty as I feel?'

'You look very nice,' Adam said honestly.

Sally squinted at Cindy. 'I don't know if you're prettier or not, Cindy. But I think you're beginning to glow. I mean really glow, like a light bulb.'

It was true. As Cindy stepped away from the fireplaces and into the shadows, she seemed to cast a shadow of her own. Her skin was emitting a faint radiance, almost as if she were radioactive. But the effect did not disturb Cindy. She appeared excited about it.

'I can be a movie star,' she said. 'I don't just have sparkle in my eyes. I have it everywhere!'

'Do I need to remind you that we are in a life and death situation here?' Sally said in a slightly squeaky voice. 'We are surrounded by stone walls, and we have nothing to eat or drink.'

Watch gestured to the ceiling. He had been staring at it for the last minute. 'I think I see a hole into the attic.'

'What are you talking about?' Adam said. 'I don't see anything.'

'And castles don't have attics,' Sally added.

'It doesn't matter what we call it,' Watch said,

removing his glasses and rubbing his eyes, before pointing to one spot on the dark stone ceiling. 'It looks like a way out to me.'

'But we could never get up there,' Cindy said.

In response, Watch jumped off the floor. But it was not an ordinary jump that an ordinary boy might make. He flew up almost two metres before coming back down.

'Wow,' he said. 'I can't wait until the next Olympics. I'll clean up on the gold medals.'

'But even if you're feeling stronger,' Sally said, 'that ceiling's ten metres high. You can't reach it.'

Adam gestured to the table where they had found the necklaces. 'But what if we take this table, break it in half, and set the two halves on top of each other? If Watch jumped from the top of that, he might be able to reach the hole in the ceiling.'

'But what about us?' Cindy asked. 'We'll still be stuck.'

Watch pulled the long white sheet off the table top. 'I'll take this with me. And once I'm up there, I'll lower it for Adam to grab. And you two can hold on to Adam's feet and I'll pull you all up at once.'

Sally smirked. 'Right. You can lift all of us at once.'

Watch spoke with a straight face. 'I think I can. I know for sure I can break this table into two pieces.

Stand aside, I don't want any of you to get hurt.'

To their amazement, they watched as Watch cut the table in half with one sharp karate chop. Or perhaps Adam was not that surprised. It had been his idea to begin with, and he was growing smarter all the time, not to mention taller.

Not needing their help, Watch piled the two pieces of the table on top of each other. Then he tucked the tablecloth in his belt, and jumped up on the very top of the tables. The gang moved back even further as he made a desperate leap for the hole in the ceiling. His first effort failed, and he came crashing back on the table top. The wood shuddered, as if he weighed a ton, and they feared the whole structure would come crashing down.

But Watch was not fazed. He made another supernatural leap, and this time he managed to catch on to the rim of the hole. In two seconds he had pulled himself up and out of view. But his head reappeared a moment later.

'This hole is like a heating duct,' he called down. 'It looks like it goes way back.' He began to feed the edge of the sheet down. 'Hurry, grab hold of the cloth. We should get out of here before Ann Templeton comes back.'

'But what if you drop us?' Sally asked as she climbed up on the split table tops.

'You're the last person who has to worry about that,' Watch said. 'You're immortal now.'

Sally frowned. 'I don't know about that. I just feel . . .' She suddenly stopped. 'Hey, is my voice getting higher?'

'Yeah,' Cindy said. 'And you're getting shorter, too.'

'You're not just getting shorter,' Adam said, studying Sally. 'You're getting younger.'

Sally was stunned. 'You mean you guys get to be older and stronger and more beautiful? And I have to turn into a baby?'

'Looks like it,' Adam said. 'But I'm not surprised the witch gave you the worst necklace. You're always rude to her.'

'Right now we don't know which necklace is good,' Watch warned them from above. 'And which necklace might be bad.'

Cindy giggled. 'I'm not worried about becoming too beautiful.'

Sally gave her a hard look. 'I think we should all be worried.'

The three of them finished climbing up on the second of the table tops. But it was only Adam – who was now taller than the rest of them by several centimetres – who could reach the sheet Watch fed down to them. For that reason, Sally and Cindy ended up holding on to Adam's legs as Watch pulled them. It was a strange sensation to have in such a strange place, Adam thought. To have his friend slowly tugging him into the air as if he were a balloon while the girls hung on to his ankles.

'That wasn't so bad,' Adam said, when they were all huddled in the hole in the ceiling. Below them they could still see the massive fireplaces, and the many burning torches. Too late he realised they should have brought one of the torches with them. The hole Watch had lifted them into looked long and dark.

'It's too bad we don't have a flashlight,' Cindy said, peering into the dark.

'I don't think I need one,' Watch said, as he put his glasses in his pocket. 'My eyes are getting more sensitive with each passing minute. I can practically see in the dark.'

They crawled forward, with Watch leading the way, Cindy at his back, Sally behind her and Adam at the rear. The tunnel did not stay even. For a while it headed down, then back up. It seemed as if they had been crawling forever when Watch finally told them to halt. Adam thought he heard metal scraping across stone, but he could not see his friend at the front of their group.

'There is some kind of grid over the space in front of us,' Watch said.

'Does it look like a way out?' Sally asked.

'It might be,' Watch said. 'But I can't see any floor below it. I think it would be risky just to jump down.' He paused and sniffed the air. 'There's this strange smell coming from below the grid.'

'What's it smell like?' Cindy asked.

'I'm not sure,' Watch said. 'But it's not a pleasant smell.'

'Can the grid support our weight?' Sally asked.

'That's another reason I stopped,' Watch said. 'It's pretty rusted. I think we had better go over it one at a time.'

'Good,' Sally said. 'You go first.'

Adam heard Watch moving on to the edge of the grid. The metal creaked loudly, and Adam realised his heart was pounding. 'Be careful, Watch,' he whispered.

'It's bending already,' Watch said in a tight voice. 'We'll be lucky if we all get across.'

'Well, don't bend it too much,' Sally said. 'I don't want to be trapped in here for the rest of my life.

Especially when it was not my idea to come here.'

'I thought you weren't going to say I told you so,' Adam said.

'It goes without saying,' Sally replied.

'I'm almost on the other side of the grid,' Watch whispered.

'How far across is it?' Adam asked.

'A long three metres,' Watch called back. He seemed to shift in the darkness ahead of them, perhaps as he was turning around. 'There, I've made it. Come, Cindy, but be sure to move slowly.'

'I'm scared,' Cindy whispered as she moved on to the grid. Once more Adam heard the creaking metal. 'What if it breaks?'

'Then you will probably fall screaming to your death,' Sally said in her most helpful manner.

'You won't die,' Adam said in an encouraging tone. 'You're a beautiful princess. The beautiful princess never dies in fairy tales.'

'The only trouble with that analogy is that Spooksville is as far from a fairy tale as you can get,' Sally said.

'Would you shut up?' Cindy hissed. 'You're making me nervous.'

'How do you think I feel?' Sally asked. 'I have to go

after you and Watch, and you two guys have bent the grid all out of shape.'

'I can hardly wait until you regress to an infant,' Cindy muttered. 'To before you could talk.'

Adam sighed. 'Isn't it amazing how we all band together at the times of greatest danger?'

Cindy made it across. They heard her celebrating on the other side with Watch. Now it was Sally's turn, and she too sounded scared as she crawled on to the grid.

'It smells like death down there,' she whispered.

'Try not to look down,' Adam said.

'Try telling that to my nose,' Sally said, obviously sweating with every move as she crawled over the grid. For Adam, she was a blur – even though he was only a metre behind her. The darkness seemed to press down upon all of them as the stink below grew stronger.

Adam thought he heard something moving far below.

Wicked licking sounds.

He prayed the grid didn't break when it was his turn.

Finally, he heard Sally call from up ahead.

'I made it,' she said. 'Just pretend you're as light as a hot air balloon, Adam, and you'll have no problem.'

'The only problem with that is I think I've gained ten kilos in the last five minutes,' Adam said, feeling for the edge of the grid. 'I wonder how old I am now.'

'I wonder when you'll stop ageing,' Watch said darkly.

Adam moved on to the grid. Immediately it sagged way down. It was unfortunate – had he been his normal size and weight, the grid would have supported him fine. Now it was creaking painfully. It sounded as if its many metal wires were desperately straining to hold together. Adam felt desperate. There was definitely something moving far below, and it wasn't human. Adam could hear the creature licking its chops, as if expecting a fresh meal. Had the witch just given him the necklace to make him into a bigger piece of meat? It was a terrifying thought.

'You're almost there,' Sally whispered on the other side.

'I've barely climbed on to the blasted thing,' Adam whispered back.

'I know that,' Sally said. 'I was just trying to be supportive.'

The grid suddenly let out a loud creak.

It dropped down half a metre.

'Adam!' Cindy screamed.

'I'm still here,' Adam gasped, trembling badly. He was clutching the grid for dear life, barely able to squeeze his fingers between the interlaced metal. Behind him, he believed, the grid had already torn loose. If he were to let go for a second, he knew he would slide off into the creature's lair. Clearly there was no chance of going back.

'You have to move carefully,' Watch advised.

'But you have to hurry up and do it,' Sally said. 'I can feel the edge of the grid on this side. It's ready to pull away.'

Adam could feel the grid slowly sinking beneath him. He feared if he moved it would just collapse. 'I think I'm stuck,' he said softly. 'I think this is it.'

'Hang on,' Sally pleaded. 'I have a plan.'

'I am all ears,' Adam whispered, feeling the sweat drip into his eyes, the perspiration sliding over his palms, making them slippery.

'Watch,' Sally said, 'do you still have the sheet you used to pull us up here with?'

'Sure.' There was a rustling in the dark. 'Are you going to throw it down to him?'

'Yes,' Sally said. 'Adam, in a moment you'll probably feel the sheet on your face or your hands. Grab hold of it and we'll pull you up.'

'Are you pulling me up or is Watch?' Adam wanted to know.

'Watch can't squeeze past Cindy to get to where I'm sitting,' Sally said. 'It will have to be me. But don't worry, I'm stronger than I look.'

'For a five year old,' Cindy muttered.

'I'm not five yet,' Sally snapped.

'You sound like it,' Cindy said.

Adam felt the edge of the sheet brush the side of his face. 'Are you sure you can hold on to me?' he asked. 'I'm going to make a grab for the sheet right now.'

'I will try my best,' Sally said. 'Cindy, you hold on to me. Watch, you hold on to Cindy.'

'We'll probably all end up going over the edge,' Cindy muttered.

'I'm going to do it now,' Adam said again.

'We're ready for you,' Sally whispered, tense.

In a single swift move, Adam let go of the grill with his right hand and grabbed at the sheet. He could feel exactly where it was, lying against his cheek, and had no trouble getting hold of it. The only problem was that his sudden move made the grill sink even deeper. He had one hand on the grill and the other on the sheet and if he let go of either he was sure he was doomed.

'Can you pull me up?' he gasped.

'Can't you crawl up?' Sally gasped back. It sounded

as if she was straining as hard as she could to hold on to him.

'I don't know,' Adam said, feeling himself slipping down, slowly, bit by bit. 'Can't you help, Watch?'

'Unfortunately the sheet isn't long enough,' Watch said. 'Whatever you're going to do, you better do it now. I don't think Sally can hold on much longer.'

'Ain't that the truth,' Sally whispered.

Using the taut sheet for support, Adam desperately tried to pull himself up. But now the grid was a mass of scary creaks. Adam could actually hear the individual wires snapping as the grid sunk so low that for all practical purposes it was hanging straight down. Far below, the waiting creature seemed to giggle. A wave of putrid air floated upwards, making Adam swoon.

'I can't hold on,' he cried.

'You have to,' Sally said. 'You can't die just when I've become immortal. I'll be bored for the rest of eternity without you to bother.'

Both the sheet and the grid were slowly slipping from his hands. 'I can't do it,' he moaned. 'I'm falling.'

'You fall and I'll kill you,' Sally said anxiously.

'You have to try harder,' Cindy pleaded.

'Just make one big jump for it,' Watch said. 'It's your only chance.'

'All right,' Adam said as he struggled for air. 'I'm doing it on the count of three. One ... Two ... Three!'

Using both his arms, Adam yanked up as hard as he could. Unfortunately, the edge of the grid was too far gone to take the shock. Still, he almost made it. He was actually able to grab hold of Sally's hand. He grabbed it hard, as if his life depended on it, which it did. But in a way it just made the situation worse.

The whole grid gave away.

It fell crashing below.

There was a high pitched cry from below – the complaint of an inhuman monster.

Adam dangled in mid air, holding on to the sheet with one hand, and Sally's hand with the other. Above him, he could feel Sally being pulled over the edge.

'I have to let go!' he cried.

'I won't let go of you!' Sally screamed.

'You must!' Adam shouted. 'You'll be pulled over the edge with me.'

'No!' Sally cried.

But Adam was right. He was already doomed, and because Sally refused to let him fall, she too was pulled over the edge. The tension broke all at once. The two of them were fighting with every last drop of strength they had, then they were suddenly falling. Into a black abyss where a pair of hungry red eyes waited to eat them alive.

Six

Cindy and Watch sat in darkness, inside and out. Neither could comprehend what had just happened. The shock was too great. Sally and Adam – their best friends – were just gone. Everything in the whole world seemed hopeless.

'Can you see anything?' Cindy whispered to Watch as he knelt at the edge of the torn grill.

'I'm having trouble seeing past you,' Watch said. 'But it wouldn't matter if I was sitting where you are sitting.'

Cindy's voice cracked. 'Because they're dead already?'

Watch spoke heavily. 'I'm afraid so. They couldn't have survived that fall, or whatever it is that's down there.'

Cindy winced. 'Do you think it's going to eat them?'

'We shouldn't think about that. They're already beyond feeling any pain.'

Cindy felt cold tears wash over her face. 'We should never have come to this evil place. I didn't want to come.'

'I know and you were right,' Watch said. 'It was my fault. I was just worried about myself.' He sighed. 'And now I have killed my best friends.'

Cindy patted his arm. 'You can't blame yourself. You just wanted to be able to see better. There's nothing wrong with that.'

Watch hung his head. 'I would trade both my eyes just to see Adam again, and to hear Sally's voice.'

After sitting for a few more minutes in mourning, they continued to crawl up the stone tunnel. There was nothing else they could do. Cindy wept as they crawled, but Watch kept his tears inside, where he kept most things.

After maybe twenty minutes of plugging along, the passageway took a sharp turn downwards. Fortunately metal rungs appeared on the sides, and they were able to hold on to them for support. Pretty soon they were climbing straight down, as if they were on a ladder. As they did so the temperature increased. A faint red glow appeared below and it seemed as if they were coming to the end of the passageway.

'We've been going down for a long time,' Cindy said as they paused to catch their breath. 'That's not good. We must have entered the witch's basement. That's where we ran into the trolls before.'

Watch nodded, hanging on to the metal rungs below her. 'I'm sure when she was talking about her boys, she meant them. Do you think it's possible she told the trolls not to eat us?'

'I doubt it,' Cindy said bitterly. 'It was she who forced us to crawl through this stone hole. I blame her for Adam and Sally's deaths. When we get out of here, I'm going straight to the police to report her.'

'The police won't do anything about it,' Watch said. 'They're afraid of Ann Templeton.' He shook his head as he stared down below them. 'I didn't think she would do anything really to hurt us.'

'Sally was wiser than all of us,' Cindy said in a sad voice. 'And I was always so mean to her.'

'You were never mean to her,' Watch said. 'You were just always annoyed with her.' He gestured to the red light below them. 'We can't hang here forever. We're going to have to try our luck with the trolls. I just wish we had a weapon of some kind.'

'Do you think you're strong enough to beat up one yet?' Cindy asked.

'No matter how strong I get,' Watch said, 'I don't think I'll be able to take a spear in the chest.' He paused and stared at her. 'You keep getting brighter. We're going to have trouble hiding you from the trolls.'

Cindy studied her body. Watch was right. With each passing minute the flesh on her arms and legs was shining with more light. Indeed, it was almost as if her skin was becoming transparent.

'If it comes down to it,' she said, 'you save yourself. You don't try to save me as well.'

Watch shook his head. 'Did you see how Sally refused to let go of Adam? She held on to him even though she knew it would kill her. How can I leave you behind?'

Cindy wiped away another tear. 'She was very brave.'

They climbed down the remainder of the passageway. The dull red light was their guide. As they climbed out, they found themselves in a wide stone cave. It stretched in both directions, and appeared empty. But the red light was only coming from the right. The left was completely dark.

'This reminds me of the Haunted Cave,' Cindy said.

'But it isn't,' Watch said. 'We can't be that deep. This tunnel was built.'

'But that's an idea,' Cindy said. 'If we could go even deeper, we could make it down to the Haunted Cave. And we know how to get out of there. We've done it before.'

'I wouldn't mind going that way,' Watch said. 'But I don't know which way it is.' He nodded in both directions. 'Do you want to go towards the light, or do you want to go towards the darkness?'

'I just want to go home,' Cindy said. But she pointed in the direction of the red glow. 'But we have to go that way. Even if you can see in the dark, I can't.'

'I agree.' Watch studied his shirt sleeve. 'The material is beginning to tear. My arms are swelling in size.'

Cindy nodded. 'You're not getting taller but you are getting more stocky. I bet pretty soon you'll be able to handle a dozen trolls.'

'Don't even say it,' Watch cautioned.

They started forward, in the direction of the red glow. It grew in brightness as the temperature continued to increase. Up ahead, through a haunting red haze, they glimpsed a huge room, a cavern of some kind, filled with metal equipment and dark moving shapes. Even as they saw the creatures, the creatures saw them. Cindy and Watch heard a bunch of loud howls, and then the creatures were running towards them.

They carried spears.

And they were not human.

Seven

In reality, Adam and Sally were not dead. Not yet.

They had fallen a long way, far enough to break every bone in their body. But they had landed on the softest of all cushions, some kind of huge net. The only trouble was that it was not a net but a sticky web. They were alive but stuck. The net's slimy fibres stuck to them like glue.

And they could hear the spider getting closer.

'It must be a big creature to make a web like this,' Adam said.

'It's probably poisonous as well,' Sally said grimly. 'Can you move?'

'Not much. How about you?'

'I'm slimed. It's all over me – in my hair, on my arms and legs. Can you see the spider yet?'

'No,' Adam said. 'But it's definitely getting closer.'

'That's bad,' Sally said.

'That's putting it mildly. Hey, I want to thank you for holding on to me when I started to fall. That was very brave of you.'

'Thank you. But I think it was awfully stupid of me.'

'Most brave acts are stupid,' Adam agreed. He had landed on his back and there he remained – no matter how hard he tried moving on to his side. The odour he had smelled from up on the grill had grown a dozen times stronger. The stink was like rotten eggs – it made it hard to breathe.

It was dark, pitch black.

They heard a slobbering sound off to their right.

They heard a munching sound off to their left.

'Oh no,' Sally cried. 'There're two spiders.'

'Maybe they'll begin to fight over us,' Adam said hopefully.

'They live together down here,' Sally said. 'They're not going to fight over us. We're doomed.'

'Don't say that. It depresses me.' Adam suddenly had an idea. 'Hey, do you have your Bic lighter in your pocket?'

'Yeah. Why?'

'We can use the flame to burn away the web,' Adam said. 'It's worth a try. Can you reach it in your pocket?'

'I think so,' Sally said as the slobbering sounds grew louder. 'But if I burn away the web, we might fall further.'

'I would rather be falling than be eaten,' Adam said.

'That's a good point.' Sally flicked on the lighter. In the light of the tiny orange flame they could see the approaching spiders. They were hideous to behold. As big as fat sheep, they had a bunch of slimy black legs and arms, and two sharp pinchers. The fire seemed to puzzle them. They stopped and stared at it with wary red eyes. But they did not turn and flee, as Adam had half hoped. Green poison dripped from their ugly mouths.

The web was erected only a metre above a black floor.

If they could burn free, they would be able to stand up and escape.

'Put the flame under the web,' Adam said. 'See if you can get it smoking.'

'I'm trying,' Sally said, manoeuvring the flame beneath the piece of web that gripped her right arm. To their delight, and surprise, it immediately caught fire, as a hair would when put close to a lighter. The web wrinkled up quickly and went back out, but in doing so it released Sally's right arm. She moved the flame to the web that gripped her left arm. The spiders made shrill angry sounds, and began to move forward again.

'Hurry,' Adam said. 'They're coming.'

'I am well aware of the fact,' Sally gasped. Her left arm came free, and then she was hanging above the floor by her feet. As she reached up to free her entangled ankles, the nearest of the spiders reached over with its pincher.

'Watch out!' Adam cried.

'Take that you ugly creature!' Sally yelled as she suddenly pulled off her shoe and smacked the spider in the face. The spider retreated a step and screamed at the other spider. In the meantime Sally freed both her feet and dropped down to the floor, actually landing on her outstretched arms. Adam only noticed then that she looked about six years old.

'You're shrinking,' he said.

Sally hurried to his side. 'Do you really want to insult me at a time like this?'

'Sorry,' Adam said.

Sally moved a flame to his wrists. 'Pull back on the web. It burns easier when it's tight.'

Adam nodded in the direction of the spiders, which had moved close to each other. It was as if the two monsters were plotting a strategy. Adam didn't want to hang around and see what surprises they came up with. He pulled the web as tight as he could as Sally licked the flame over the slimy thread.

'I should carry a lighter myself,' he said. 'It's saved our lives a few times already.'

'You get three in a packet for less than two dollars,' Sally agreed.

Suddenly the spiders turned back in their direction. As a team the monsters rushed them. Adam struggled uselessly, just covering himself with more web.

'Get a stick!' he cried. 'They're coming.'

'We're in a dungeon. There are no sticks.'

'Then get a stone!' Adam shouted as the monster moved within three metres. 'Anything! They're going to sting me with their poison venom!'

Sally looked round. A couple of loose bricks lay against a nearby wall. Grabbing them she whirled on the spiders and let fly with the stones. One hit the closest spider in the eyes. The second brick struck the other spider's stinger. It broke it, in fact – the spider let out a loud miserable screech. Sally returned to melting the web as the spiders retreated to the far corner.

'I owe you one,' Adam said.

'You owe me a dozen,' Sally replied.

A minute later Adam was free of the sticky web, and

able to stand upright on the floor beside Sally. They realised that they were not in a real dungeon. There was a wide tunnel off to the right that led out of the spiders' lair. As they ran away from the web, Sally turned and shouted back at the spiders.

'Next time I'm going to bring bug spray!'

The tunnel led to a stone ladder, which was carved into the wall. The tunnel also continued further along, but they both thought it was a good idea to head upwards. But Sally was shocked to find she could hardly climb the ladder.

'It's because you're getting shorter,' Adam said as he came up behind her.

'I know that. You don't have to keep rubbing it in.' She paused. 'Hey, your voice sounds a lot deeper.'

'Yeah. I sound like a teenager.'

'Don't be coy,' Sally said. 'You sound like a man.'

At the top of the stone ladder – which had been a long climb – they came to another stone tunnel. But this one was different from the others. Lit with a haunting violet light, it was much cleaner than the place they had left behind. There was also a pleasant smell to it, as if someone had recently burned incense. Moving in the direction of the wonderful light, Adam felt as if they were entering a place of ancient magic.

'I have never seen this coloured light before,' Adam said.

'Yes. It's enchanting.' Sally paused. 'We have to be careful of another trap.'

They entered a large dome-shaped chamber, filled with bushes and trees and grass. The violet glow seemed to come out of the ceiling itself. There was even a circular pond in the room. And sitting in the middle of the tiny lake was a girl of about ten, with long curly black hair. She opened her eyes as they entered, as if coming out of deep meditation. Her eyes were as green as Ann Templeton's, but the smile on her incredible face was filled only with kindness.

'Hello,' she said in a gentle voice. 'My name is Mireen. Who are you?'

Eight

Cindy and Watch were captured by a gang of big ugly trolls. The beasts carried spears and swords, arrows and knives. They dragged Cindy and Watch kicking into the large cavern where still more trolls slaved over clanging machines that made heaven only knew what. All the trolls stopped to stare as Cindy and Watch were forced to stand beside a pool of boiling lava. It was the lava that gave off the red light, and perhaps helped fuel the big machines.

Cindy and Watch exchanged worried looks. They had no doubt they would be thrown into the lava, or else cooked over it.

'Can you break free?' Cindy asked in a quiet voice.

Watch shook his head. 'There're too many of them.'

'Silence!' one of the trolls shouted, putting the tip

of his sword to Watch's throat. 'No one gave you permission to speak.'

'I'm sorry,' Watch said. 'I didn't know you trolls could speak English.'

The comment seemed to amuse the monster, for he smiled widely, as slobber fell over his breastplate of stainless steel. Like his partners, his face was blunt, his thick nose hairy, and his skin scaled, like that of a lizard. But he was bigger than his partners, and maybe that was why he was their leader. He strode in front of them as if they were his trophies.

'Our boss has taught us to speak your human language,' the troll said. 'She says we will need it in the future, when we go out into the world, and make all of you our slaves.'

'It won't happen,' Cindy said. 'We humans have a group called the Marines. They'll kick your ugly behinds.'

The troll paused in his pacing. 'Who are these Marines?'

'They are the proud and the few,' Watch said. 'They have much better weapons than spears and swords. If I were you I would stay down here. The Marines would wipe you all out in one day.'

'But are these Marines human?' the troll asked.

'They are human soldiers,' Cindy said. 'They always win, and don't quit until the enemy has been defeated.' She added hopefully, 'They are good friends of ours. If you hurt us, they won't like that.'

'Yeah, you should just let us go,' Watch said. 'If you eat us alive, our friends will become your enemies.'

The troll sniggered at their threat. 'Nobody is going to save you here. We will have you for dinner, that is certain. It only remains to see how you are to be cooked.' He added, 'My name is Belfart, by the way.'

'I'm Watch and this is Cindy,' Watch said.

'Pleased to meet you, Belfart,' Cindy said. 'Do you have to eat us? If you let us go, we promise to bring you back fresh steak from the grocery store.'

Belfart scoffed. 'We don't even like cows. Human meat is much more tasty.' He lightly poked Cindy's side with the tip of his sword. 'I think I will eat you myself.'

Cindy shoved aside his sword and spat on him. 'Then kill us both and get it over with. Your bad breath is giving me a headache.'

Belfart wiped away the spit with his long purple tongue. 'Not so fast. We have to have a vote. We are a democratic group of trolls.' Belfart turned to the gathered monsters. To Cindy and Watch's surprise, he continued to speak in English, perhaps to torture them all the more. 'How do we cook them?' Belfart called out.

Clearly it was an important question, at least as far as the trolls were concerned. Immediately half a dozen of the monsters yelled out that the humans should be roasted. Just as quickly another half dozen said that the humans should be broiled. Still others wanted them boiled, while a couple of trolls wanted them skinned alive. Soon there was a big argument going on, and Belfart had lost all control of his group. Indeed, several of the trolls drew their swords and looked ready to die to defend their choice of how the humans should be cooked. Cindy looked over at Watch and sighed.

'This is worse than being eaten,' Cindy said.

'I don't know about that,' Watch said. 'They can argue as long as they want as far as I'm concerned.'

'We need a plan of action,' Cindy said.

'I was going to suggest that they at least kill us before they eat us.'

'That's no plan. If Adam and Sally were here, they wouldn't give up without a fight.'

'If I try to fight them all,' Watch said, 'we'll both end up dead.'

'I have an idea,' Cindy said. She called over to the

troll leader. 'Belfart! There's something I must tell you guys before you make a decision as to how we are to be cooked.'

Belfart shouted for the group to shut up, and because it was one of the humans who wanted to speak, they did. Cindy addressed the group as a whole.

'Now I know you are hungry,' she said. 'And I know nothing would taste better to you than roasted human right now.'

'Boiled human would taste better!' a troll shouted.

'Grilled!' another troll yelled.

'Satéed!' a troll at the back screamed.

'Whatever!' Cindy yelled back. 'You want to eat us and I can understand that. But there's something we've got to tell you.' She paused for effect. 'Me and my partner are sick. If you eat us, you'll get sick too.'

Belfart took a step closer and sniffed her. 'You don't smell sick.'

'But I am,' she said. 'So is Watch. We have the measles.'

'I already had the measles,' Watch said.

'And now you have them again,' Cindy said quickly. 'In case you think we're lying, you just have to wait a few hours and we'll get these red spots all over our bodies.'

Belfart seemed unconvinced. 'But we're hungry now.'

'Yes,' Cindy said patiently. 'But you don't want to get sick. The measles are awful. If you catch them, all the girl trolls won't even want to get near you.'

That sent a stir through the room. Belfart put his scaly hand to his fat jaw and appeared thoughtful. 'How long does it take you to get the red spots?' he asked.

'We'll have them within six hours,' Cindy said confidently. 'Wait that long and you'll see.'

'Let's wait and then fry them!' a troll shouted.

'We wait and then we bake them!' another yelled.

'No!' a bunch at the back said. 'We put them in the microwave!'

'Where did they get a microwave?' Watch muttered.

'Shut up all of you!' Belfart screamed. 'We will first lock them up and see if they get sick. If they don't, then we can argue about how to cook them.'

Cindy leaned over and whispered in Watch's ear. 'I have just bought us time.'

Watch nodded grimly. 'But they're just going to come for us later.'

Nine

'I'm Adam. This is Sally,' Adam said to the strange girl. 'What are you doing here?'

'This is where I have always been.' Mireen stood up in her place at the centre of the pond. With a slight nod of her head a series of stones appeared in the water, providing a pathway for her across the pond. As she approached, Adam noticed she was wearing a dark grey cloak, similar in design to Ann Templeton's. Mireen asked, 'What are you doing here?'

'We've been trapped in this castle by the witch,' Sally said angrily. 'Has she trapped you as well?'

Mireen appeared puzzled. Her face, although very beautiful, was as pale as Ann Templeton's. It seemed almost as if it were made of marble; it did not have a blemish on it.

'Who is this witch you speak of?' she asked.

'Ann Templeton,' Adam explained. 'She gave us these magic necklaces and now we can't get them off. We can't find our way out of here either.'

Mireen smiled. 'Ann Templeton isn't a witch. Why do you call her that?'

'What would you call her?' Sally demanded in her now squeaky voice. Sally was down to the size of a four year old. In a sense, Adam was not doing much better. Sally was wrong – he was no longer a teenager. In fact, he seemed to have skipped his twenties altogether. He was getting really old, in his mid-thirties at least. Pretty soon he would have arthritis and not even be able to walk properly, like most older adults.

'I call her Mother,' Mireen said.

They were stunned. 'You're Ann Templeton's daughter?' Sally asked.

'Yes. Don't I look like her daughter?'

Mireen did indeed resemble the witch. Yet there was an otherworldly character to her face that even Ann Templeton didn't have.

'Who's your father?' Adam asked.

A trace of sorrow touched Mireen's face. 'His name is supposed to be Faltoreen. But I have never met him.'

'Why not?' Sally asked. 'Did your mother kill him?'

'No,' Mireen said. 'Why would my mother kill him?'

'She's trying to kill us,' Sally said.

'No, my father is alive and well,' Mireen said. 'He just doesn't live here.'

'Where does he live?' Adam asked.

'On another planet,' Mireen said. 'Circling another star.'

Sally laughed out loud. 'I hate to tell you this, Mireen, but that's an old excuse. Your father just took off one day and didn't bother coming back. Not that I can say I blame him after seeing the creeps that are running around this castle.'

'I'm not too sure of that,' Adam said. 'Remember how Bum said that Ann Templeton and her family were connected to star people who live in the Pleiades star group?'

'Pleiades,' Mireen said, her face shining with pleasure at the sound of the word. 'That is it. That is the name of the star group where my father lives.'

'But you say you've never seen him,' Sally said. 'How come he never visits you? Doesn't he have a spaceship?'

'He commands a whole fleet of ships,' Mireen said. 'But my mother says it is not time for him to return here.'

'I don't know if you can believe everything your mother says,' Sally said.

'We have explained how she's trapped us here,' Adam said carefully. 'You can understand that we have good reason to distrust her.' He paused. 'But you're more our age. We would like to trust you.'

'But you're much older than me, Adam,' Mireen said. 'And Sally is much younger.'

'We weren't when we started out the day,' Sally muttered.

'What Sally means is that these necklaces that we can't get off are making me older and her younger,' Adam explained. 'They have magic stones in them.' He paused. 'But maybe you know how to get them off?'

'I can certainly try,' Mireen said, stepping closer. Touching Adam's necklace, she closed her eyes and went perfectly still. Under her breath she whispered a chant. Adam and Sally didn't understand a word of it. Then Mireen opened her eyes and tried to lift off the necklace. But once more the gold strand would not pass over his head. Mireen added, 'These are bound with powerful magic. I can't undo it, but I know my mother could.'

'If she was ever in the mood,' Sally muttered.

'Your mother said these necklaces will not come off until we find our way out of here,' Adam explained. 'For that reason, we have to get out of here right away.

Soon Sally will be in nappies and I'll be in my forties and unable to get around properly.' He paused. 'You do know how to get out of here, don't you?'

Mireen blinked. 'No.'

'But you live here,' Sally said, exasperated. 'You said so yourself.'

'But I have never been outside,' Mireen said.

'Why not?' Adam asked.

'My mother says it is not time for that either,' Mireen explained. 'She says the outside is a cruel and barbaric place.'

'What about the trolls in your basement?' Sally asked. 'I've run into them before. They're not exactly warm and fuzzy kinds of characters.'

'They are always very polite to me,' Mireen said.

'What about the huge poisonous spiders?' Sally asked, trying again. 'Don't tell me they like you as well.'

'No, they can be troublesome. You just have to stay out of their way.'

'Look,' Adam said. 'We don't care if you like trolls and spiders. We just want to find our friends and get out of this place.'

'Where are your friends?' Mireen asked.

'We don't know,' Sally said. 'We got separated

above the spiders' lair. The trolls could have got them by now for all we know.'

'The trolls are not easy to control when they're hungry,' Mireen admitted. 'Come, we'll look for them. And after we find them, we'll search for a way out.'

Ten

Belfart locked Cindy and Watch in an unpleasant cell. It was damp and smelly, and there was a skeleton chained to a wall in the corner. From the size of it, they figured the trolls had feasted on a kid their age earlier in the year. Perhaps as a favour, Belfart had chained them to the wall in the opposite corner.

'I wonder if it was James Hatterfield,' Watch mused. 'He was supposed to have disappeared in the vicinity of this castle.'

'Did you go to school with him?' Cindy asked. She had yet to start school in Spooksville.

'Yeah, he was in the same grade as Sally and me. He was a nice guy but kind of chubby.' Watch added, 'The trolls probably liked that about him.'

'I still can't get over how you guys take it for granted that people disappear in this town,' Cindy said.

Watch shrugged. 'It happens every other day. You get used to it.'

Cindy sighed. 'My mother's going to be really upset if I get eaten by a troll. She wanted me home early for dinner.'

'I haven't had dinner with my mother in years,' Watch said quietly.

Cindy studied him in the poor light. Watch seldom talked about his family. All that Cindy knew was that they were scattered across the country. She did not know why.

'You miss her, don't you?' she asked.

Watch lowered his head. 'Yeah, I do. I miss my father and sister too.' He raised his head. 'But I can't worry about them now.'

'We can talk about them later if you like,' Cindy said gently. 'But first we have to get out of here. Can you break your chains?'

'I was just about to try.' Watch took a deep breath and tugged at the binds as hard as he could. But even though the iron pin that held the chains to the wall groaned as it moved slightly, the chains refused to come loose. Watch finally gave up straining. 'Let's wait a while longer,' he suggested. 'I keep getting stronger. I might be able to pop them loose before the trolls come back for us.'

Cindy nodded at the iron door. 'But will you be able to get through that? I don't know if ten super-strong men could.'

Watch paused. 'I think I hear someone coming.'

'But it hasn't been six hours,' Cindy said. 'It's been less than an hour.'

'Maybe trolls don't know how to tell the time,' Watch said.

Belfart appeared on the other side of the thick metal bars. He had a large black key with him, which he used to open the door. Stepping inside, he set aside his sword and spear, like he wanted it to be a friendly meeting.

'It hasn't been six hours,' Cindy said quickly. 'You can't eat us yet.'

Belfart waved away her remark. 'We'll get to that later. I've come to make you a proposition.'

'What kind of proposition?' Cindy asked.

'I want more information about these Marines,' Belfart said. 'You give it to me and I'll make sure you die painlessly.'

'I have a better idea,' Cindy said. 'We tell everything you could ever want to know about the Marines and you help us escape.'

Belfart shook his head. 'That's not possible. The

boys are all riled up. If I let you go, they'll eat me instead. But if you do help me, at the very least I can make sure you're not satéed.'

'That's something,' Watch said.

'That's ridiculous,' Cindy complained. 'Why should I care if I'm satéed or barbecued if I'm dead? I'm not telling you anything about the Marines unless you let us both go. It's that simple.'

'Why do you want to know about them anyway?' Watch asked.

Belfart scratched his hairy nose and paced the cell. 'This is kind of hard for me to admit, being a troll and all. But when you were talking about the Marines, something stirred deep inside me. They sound like a powerful group of boys. "The proud and the few." I kind of liked the sound of that.' He paused. 'This is strictly confidential, you understand, but I would like to find out how I could join their organisation.'

'The Marines would never accept a troll,' Watch said.

Belfart stopped pacing. His ugly face seemed to fall. 'Are you sure?'

Cindy spoke quickly. 'What Watch means is they would never accept a troll with bad breath. It's against article two-three-zero of their secret code. But if you learn to brush your teeth, gargle and floss regularly, they would be happy to take you on board.'

Watch was not so sure. 'Are you certain, Cindy? How would they find a uniform that fits Belfart?'

'I'm positive,' Cindy said, catching Watch's eye. 'In fact, why don't you give Belfart that brochure you have on the Marines.'

'Which brochure is that?' Watch asked.

'The one in your back pocket,' Cindy said. 'If Belfart unlocks your chains, you can get it for him. Can't you, Watch?'

Watch finally caught on. His new muscles seemed to be making him a little slower upstairs. 'Yes, I remember now. My brochure on how to get into the Marines. I would be happy to give it to you if you just loosen these chains a little, Belfart.'

Belfart paused. 'This wouldn't be some kind of trick, would it?' he asked.

'What can Watch do to you?' Cindy asked. 'He's just a boy, while you're a big strong handsome troll.'

Belfart puffed himself up. 'So you think I'm handsome?'

'I noticed it right away,' Cindy said.

Belfart studied her a bit closer. 'Why is it that your skin is glowing?'

'It's another sign of measles,' Cindy muttered. 'Just open Watch's chains and let him show you the best way to sign up to serve your country.'

Belfart nodded enthusiastically as he took his keys back out. 'I'd like to get out of here, and travel a bit. Don't get me wrong, Ann Templeton is great to work for. It's just that I'm tired of all the back-stabbing that goes on around here. I mean, just last week an old friend tried to put a knife in me while I was taking my afternoon nap.'

'There's nothing worse than a disloyal troll,' Cindy said sympathetically.

'You'll find this brochure very informative,' Watch promised as Belfart worked on the lock.

'Could you read it to me?' Belfart asked. 'I sometimes have trouble understanding promotional literature.'

'I'll make sure the information gets into your head,' Watch said when his hands were free. He nodded to the chains on his feet. 'Could you unlock those as well? It's hard for me to get to my back pocket while I'm still pinned to the wall.'

Belfart was in a trusting mood. 'No problem,' he said, bending over. 'You guys are more polite than most of the humans we've seen around here. Most of them refuse to stop screaming and begging. It gets on your nerves after a while. You just want to put them in the pot even if it means in the end you don't get the meat flavoured exactly the way you want it.'

'We are very polite,' Cindy said, nodding to Watch.

'You can trust us with your life,' Watch said as he brought his hands up above Belfart's head. The troll had just snapped the ankle chains free, and was glancing up, when Watch brought his fists down hard. Watch was strong enough by now. It was a loud blow. He almost took off the troll's head.

Belfart crumpled unconscious to the floor.

'Grab his keys,' Cindy said, excited. 'Undo my chains. We can be out of here before he wakes up.'

Watch reached for the keys. 'I have a better idea. Let's take him as a hostage.'

'Do you think you can handle him?' Cindy asked.

'If I keep a sword to his throat I can. He may even know a way out of here.'

Cindy looked down at the sleeping troll and frowned. 'I don't know. He doesn't look as if he gets out much.'

Eleven

The power of the magic necklaces was still at work. Adam was now an old man, at least fifty, and Sally was as small as a two year old. Adam had to carry her in his arms as Mireen led them through the castle, just so they could both keep up. Sally did not like being carried. She kept bothering Adam about his nappy remark.

'I'm not wearing them,' she said. 'I don't care how young I get. And you're certainly not changing them.'

'You might have to wear them,' Adam said. 'Look at you now. You've slipped out of your pants. Your shirt is the only thing covering you up.'

'I like this shirt,' Sally said. 'It's one of my favourites. But I mean what I say. I don't want some senile old goat taking care of me when I'm a baby.'

'I'm not senile yet,' Adam said.

'But you're getting close. Your hair's almost white.'

'It's silver, it's not white.'

'See,' Sally said. 'You're too far gone to know there's no difference.'

'Do you two always argue like this?' Mireen asked.

'Yes,' Sally said.

'No,' Adam said, then sighed. 'Sometimes. Look, do you know where you're going?'

'I know my way around the castle,' Mireen explained. 'But it's a big place, and I have no idea where your friends might be. I'm just looking everywhere.'

'Let's try searching the trolls' basement,' Sally said. 'Knowing Cindy and Watch, they're probably being roasted alive as we speak.'

'We can look there if you'd like,' Mireen said, stopping in front of a stone wall and muttering a few words of magic. There didn't seem to be many real doors in the place. Mireen was forever materialising passageways out of nothing. This time was no exception. A narrow doorway suddenly appeared before them and they hurried inside. Glancing over his shoulder, Adam saw the wall reappear where it had been. The path before them was dark but that did not seem to bother Mireen.

'Do you have any idea where your mother is?' he asked Mireen.

'If she is in the castle, she is hiding from even me,' Mireen said, troubled. 'I can usually find her just by thinking about her.'

'She might be testing you as well as us,' Adam said.

'Testing me?' Mireen said. 'I don't understand.'

'The witch . . .' Sally began. 'I mean, your mother said she was testing us with these necklaces.'

Mireen continued to appear troubled. 'Are all the kids outside afraid of my mother?'

'Most of them,' Adam admitted. 'She is supposed to have murdered a lot of them.'

Mireen laughed, but it sounded forced. 'My mother would never murder anyone. How can those kids be so foolish?'

'They've lost too many brothers and sisters?' Sally suggested.

Mireen shook her head. 'My mother's powerful, but she never abuses her power. There is a reason behind everything she does.'

'I hope you're right,' Adam muttered.

'Tell me what it's like on the outside?' Mireen asked.

'In Spooksville or in the world as a whole?' Sally asked. 'The reason I ask is because Spooksville is unlike any other place. Other cities don't have castles like this.'

'What do you do each day for fun?' Mireen asked.

'Before I moved here from Kansas City,' Adam said, 'I used to go swimming and fishing in the lake. Sometimes I would ride my bike and play baseball.'

'But since he got here he's been struggling to stay alive,' Sally said. 'We wrestle with ghosts, fight with aliens, destroy cold creatures from the past, get lost in haunted caves. We have all kinds of fun. It's a laugh a minute. You should play with us some time. You're more than welcome.'

'Perhaps some day I will,' Mireen said in a soft, maybe sad, voice.

'Do you have anyone to play with?' Adam asked gently.

'I have learned to play in my imagination,' Mireen said. 'My mother says that's the best place to play. There are more possibilities inside us, she says, than outside.'

'Hmm,' Adam muttered thoughtfully. 'Those are beautiful words.'

'And of absolutely no use to us now,' Sally said. 'Sorry, Mireen, but if we don't get these necklaces off soon, you won't be playing with us. You'll be baby-sitting us.'

'I will do everything I can to help you,' Mireen promised.

They passed from their narrow passageway into a wider tunnel lit with a sober red glow. In the distance they could hear frantic steps, two or three people running their way. But beyond that, a little further away, they could hear what sounded like a small army of trolls in battle gear. Adam strained his eyes in the gloomy light. One of the approaching figures seemed to be glowing. Adam realised who he was looking at.

'Cindy!' Adam called. 'Watch! We're over here!'

Twelve

Cindy and Watch caught up with them a few minutes later. Adam was surprised to see they had a troll with them. Watch guarded the monster by holding the sword to the troll's throat, but for his part the troll didn't seem to mind. In fact, he offered his hand.

'I'm Belfart,' he said. 'I'm a Marine.'

'I'm Mireen,' Mireen said to Cindy and Watch.

'She's the witch's daughter,' Sally said.

'Wow,' Watch said. 'I didn't know Ann Templeton was even married.'

'Belfart wants to be a Marine,' Cindy explained impatiently. 'But let's drop these introductions. We can do that later. What are you guys doing here? You're supposed to be dead.'

'Don't count the dead in this town until you've seen the bodies,' Sally said.

'I'll never do it again.' Cindy hugged them both. 'I'm just so happy to see you guys are all right.'

'Yeah, this is great,' Watch said with unexpected emotion in his voice. He reached over and hugged them too. But they just ended up crushing little Sally. She pushed them away.

'This is not great,' she said. 'I can hardly walk any more. And you, Watch, you look ready to burst out of your clothes. Adam's got the same problem, mind you. Mireen had to find him a sheet to keep him covered. And you, Cindy, you're so radiant you're on the verge of disappearing.'

'I know that,' Cindy said. 'We have to get these necklaces off.'

'First we have to get away from these trolls who are chasing us,' Watch said. 'We just escaped from their prison and they're really mad.'

'I'll talk to them,' Mireen said. 'They won't hurt you.'

'If I may beg to differ, my lady,' Belfart said. 'You won't calm them down by talking to them. I know my boys. They want human meat and they want it now. They don't even care how it's cooked, and that tells you how upset they are.'

'But can't you calm them down?' Mireen asked.

Belfart rubbed his head and glanced at Cindy and Watch. 'They think I helped these guys escape. They're hot for my bones as well.'

'Can't you lead us into a secret passageway?' Adam asked Mireen.

'Can't she just lead us out of here?' Cindy asked.

'That's what I asked,' Sally muttered.

'There is no secret passageway here,' Mireen said. 'We have to go further up the tunnel.'

'But we just came out of a secret passageway,' Adam said.

'Yes, but it was a one way passageway,' Mireen explained. 'Come, let's hurry. I know a place to take you where you will be safe.'

'Will there be a bottle there for Sally?' Cindy teased.

'Shut up,' Sally grumbled.

They ran up the tunnel as best as they could, but the trolls continued to gain on them. Adam had handed Sally to Watch to carry, but he was still slowing down the group. He definitely had arthritis now. His knees and hips ached, plus breathing was hard. Running a few steps winded him. He estimated he was seventy years old.

Cindy was also having trouble running. It was as if her disappearing feet couldn't get a grip on the ground.

She bounced in the air as she ran, as if she were on the moon.

Behind them, the troll army became visible, with dozens of burning eyes.

'The boys are full of life tonight,' Belfart said wistfully. 'Better get us to a passageway quick, my lady, or they'll tear us apart in this very tunnel.'

'We still have a way to go,' Mireen said anxiously.

'You're a witch's daughter,' Sally said. 'Do some witchcraft. Scare them away.'

Mireen stopped. 'There is a spell I know that might slow them down.' She put her hands to her head as if she was thinking deeply. 'But I can't remember exactly how it goes.'

'Is there a pocket witch dictionary or something you can look in?' Sally asked.

'Let her concentrate,' Adam said. 'There's no hurry, Mireen. Take your time.'

'But don't take too much of it,' Belfart said.

Cindy nodded to Watch. 'He's definitely Marine material.'

'I've got it!' Mireen said, excited. 'I think I've got it. All of you, stand back.'

They cleared a space for her as she stepped into the centre of the tunnel and faced in the direction of the approaching army. The trolls were clearly visible now, and they were not a pleasant sight. They already had their swords drawn, and even the sight of their boss's daughter didn't slow them down a step. Unless Mireen was able to stop them, Adam realised, the horde would be on them in a minute.

'Katuu Shamar Plean!' Mireen called as she lifted her arms.

Nothing happened.

'Try another one,' Sally said anxiously.

Mireen closed her eyes and drew in a deep breath. She raised her arms. 'Katuu Shamar Klean!'

The tunnel burst into fire. The flames exploded out of thin air in front of the attacking trolls. Adam was not sure if any of them got burned, but the whole bunch of them definitely got scared. They turned and ran the other way.

But then the flames went out.

'Do it again!' Sally called from her place in Watch's strong arms.

'I can only do it once,' Mireen said wearily as she turned and stumbled up the tunnel. 'That was enough to drain all my power.'

'That won't hold them for long, my lady,' Belfart said. 'Best we find that secret passageway quickly.'

Belfart was right. Already a few of the trolls looked as if they were having second thoughts about leaving their dinner. Several were still staring their way, calling to their partners to come back. Adam braced himself for another exhausting dash. If the trolls didn't get him, he thought, a heart attack would. He had never realised how miserable it could be to grow old.

They hurried up the tunnel, Adam staggering, Cindy bouncing, Mireen stumbling, and Sally complaining. Only Watch seemed in good shape. In a sense, his necklace had done him the most good. At least he seemed to be experiencing the fewest side effects.

Behind them, the trolls regrouped and started after them again.

'Is it much further?' Adam gasped.

'We're almost there,' Mireen called. 'I think.'

Another exhausting five minutes went by. Adam struggled on as best as he could, but invariably he began to fall behind the others. But faint whistling sounds in the dark gave him an unexpected burst of energy. The trolls were firing arrows at him, trying to cut him down. Adam swore he would not give them the pleasure.

Up ahead, Mireen stopped and faced the stone wall. The gang gathered around her. Adam was just coming up when an opening appeared out of nowhere. As a group, they poured into the magic doorway. Arrows bounced on the stone above their heads.

'Close it!' Adam cried when they were all inside.

'Weeta!' Mireen shouted over her shoulder.

The doorway vanished. The trolls were stopped.

The gang staggered through the passageway.

Then they emerged into a large room.

Adam recognised it. The room with the hourglass.

The witch was waiting for them.

Thirteen

'So you still haven't found your way out,' Ann Templeton said, her back to the magic hourglass. The light of the stardust shone about her, creating a coloured aura over her head. To Adam she didn't even look human any more, more like a powerful being from another solar system. Her green eyes glittered as she spoke, as if with strong emotion, even though her voice remained calm. She added, 'What does this mean?'

'It means you need more doors in this place,' Sally said.

Ann Templeton smiled and gestured in the direction of the hallway through which they had first entered the room. 'Why don't you go that way?' she asked. 'See what you can find?'

Adam took a weary step forward. 'We know we would find nothing. You have us locked in a maze.

There is no way out. Even your daughter does not know how to get out of this place.'

Mireen also took a step forward. 'Why are you torturing these nice kids?'

'Be silent, Mireen,' Ann Templeton said. 'Watch, listen, learn.'

'No,' Mireen replied. 'I can't remain silent while my friends are in danger.'

Her daughter's defiance seemed to surprise Ann Templeton, even to anger her. But she quickly mastered her emotions. She spoke in a quiet voice.

'You just met these people. How can you call them friends?'

Mireen shook her head. 'It's just how I feel. I like them, I care about them.' She added reluctantly, 'I can't let you hurt them.'

Ann Templeton smiled coldly. 'Do I hurt them? I did not ask them to come here. They wanted to. They wanted to see what my castle was like. Now they know. Now they're happy.'

'I wouldn't exactly say that I'm a happy one year old,' Sally muttered.

Adam spoke with effort. He still hadn't caught his breath from the mad dash up the tunnel. 'You must know that we're running out of time. Soon Cindy will disappear, Sally will turn back into an egg, and I'll die of old age. If we've failed your test, then we've failed it. We don't know what else we can do to get out of here.'

'Why, Adam, I'm disappointed in you,' Ann Templeton said in a serious voice. 'You have not even tried to get out of here. Sure, you've crawled into this hole, and explored this cave, and searched through this passageway. But that is not how you escape from a trap. To do that you have to look at how you got into the trap. Then you will know what to do.'

'But Mother,' Mireen pleaded. 'Adam told you. They don't have time for this. They're dying.'

'How do you feel, Watch?' Ann Templeton asked. 'Do you feel like you're dying?'

'No ma'am,' he replied. 'I feel stronger than ever.'

'Somehow I'm not surprised.' Ann Templeton lowered her head and closed her eyes, as if thinking deeply. Then she raised her head and stared at each one of them, including her daughter. Finally she spoke, and there was great power in her words, as if she were passing judgment on them. 'I will leave you now. You will pass the test or you will fail it. It is up to you.' She turned away. 'Come, Mireen.'

'No,' her daughter said flatly. 'I'm staying here with my friends. If you won't help them, maybe I can.'

Ann Templeton paused and studied her. But she seemed unconcerned with her daughter's disobedience. 'You're old enough to make up your own mind, Mireen.' She gestured to Belfart. 'Come with me.'

'See you guys later,' he said casually. 'If I'm lucky. Remember that brochure on the Marines. I still think they could use a few good trolls.'

And with that Ann Templeton and Belfart vanished into the wall.

Fourteen

'She sure makes a stunning exit, doesn't she?' Sally said in her baby's voice.

Adam stepped up to the hourglass and leaned against it for support. 'We're back where we started from.'

'No,' Cindy disagreed, in a voice they could hardly hear. They could see right through her now. Her words were like a ghost's whispers. 'We're worse off than when we started. We have only a few minutes left to figure out what to do.'

Adam sighed. 'I just wish I could think more clearly. I'm definitely getting senile. Does anyone have any suggestions?'

'The witch did not have to meet us here,' Watch said. 'But she did, and I think she did so as a favour.'

'I could do with less of her favours,' Sally said.

'You misunderstand me,' Watch said. 'I think she was trying to give us a hint. Let's think about what she said. "But that is not how you escape from a trap. To do that you have to look at how you got into the trap. Then you will know what to do." ' Watch paused. 'The key must be in those words.'

'But how did we get in this trap?' Adam asked. 'We walked over and walked inside and we were trapped.'

'No,' Cindy said. 'The door closed behind us as soon as we stepped inside, but I don't think we were trapped until we put on the necklaces. The witch said as much earlier.'

'I think we have to go further back than that,' Watch said. 'I think we have to ask ourselves why we came here.'

'For the usual reasons,' Sally said. 'Because we were bored and stupid.'

'We may have been bored,' Adam said. 'But the thing that decided us to come here was Watch's failing eyesight.'

'And Watch is the only one who is not suffering right now,' Mireen said. 'Mother pointed that out. She said that it did not surprise her.'

'But why isn't Watch suffering like the rest of us?' Cindy said. 'Maybe that's the key to this big test.'

'I think he's going to suffer when he tries to buy some new clothes,' Sally said. 'And he looks like the Incredible Hulk.'

'Cindy's on to something,' Adam interrupted. 'We came here because of Watch. Actually, Watch was the only one who had a genuine reason to come. He needed help with his eyesight and now his eyesight is better. Also, he was the first one to put on the necklace. He trusted that he would be all right. He had faith.'

'Thank you for the sermon,' Sally said. 'But how does this help us get these stupid necklaces off?'

'I think it gives us a clue as to why we can't get them off,' Adam said. 'I put the necklace on because I wanted something for nothing. I wanted to be more mature.'

'And I wanted to be prettier,' Cindy agreed. 'Even though I was pretty enough to begin with.'

'And humble enough,' Sally added.

'The point is the three of us were fine to begin with,' Adam said. 'We didn't have anything wrong with us. But still we put on the necklaces.' He paused. 'Could the test be just that. That we took something we didn't need. That we were fine the way we were and we still wanted something more.'

107

Cindy nodded. 'I think that's it. The test is inside. It's there that we failed it.'

'But how do we get these stupid necklaces off?' Sally demanded.

Mireen spoke up. 'My mother has a saying. It's always been one of my favourites. She says that the things we crave the most destroy us the quickest.'

'Interesting,' Adam said thoughtfully. 'I certainly don't crave maturity any more.'

'And I don't crave beauty any more,' Cindy said.

They all looked at little Sally.

'Well, I'm tired of being a baby if that's what you want to hear,' she said. 'Now I have just one tiny question. I've asked it before. How do we get these necklaces off?'

They stared at each other, searching for an answer.

'Why don't you just try taking them off?' Mireen suggested.

'We tried that already,' Sally said. 'Many times. They won't come off.'

'Try now,' Mireen said gently.

Adam tried first.

Without effort, the necklace passed over his head.

Cindy quickly pulled off her necklace.

Sally took off hers. She smiled a big baby smile.

They all stared at Watch. He fingered his ruby.

'You don't have to take it off,' Adam said. 'It isn't hurting you.'

Watch was doubtful. 'But how can I want to be special when you guys aren't allowed to be? It's not fair.' He pulled the necklace over his head. 'I got by before. I can get by again. Even if I do go blind, there are worse things.'

Mireen went over and put her hand on Watch's chest. 'You're a great person. You have a big heart.'

Watch blushed. 'Thank you.'

'I think this may be the start of something,' Cindy said.

'Excuse me,' Sally spoke up. 'Are you guys forgetting a minor detail? We have removed the necklaces and maybe we have stopped ageing and shrinking and disappearing. But we are still far from back to normal.'

'I think I may have an answer to that problem,' Adam said, touching the hourglass once more. 'Mireen, has your mother ever spoken about this hourglass?'

'Very seldom,' Mireen said. 'But she did once say its power reached to the stars. That even the stars' paths through the heavens could be influenced by it.'

'What does that mean?' Sally said.

109

'We already know,' Adam said. 'We were shown on the other side of the Secret Path. This hourglass controls the flow of time.'

'But you said we can't mess with it,' Cindy said. 'You said it could destroy our world.'

'I said we couldn't destroy it,' Adam corrected. 'We destroyed the other one in the other dimension. But what if we perform an experiment. What if we put the necklaces back on, and turn the hourglass upside down, and then see what happens.'

'What will happen?' Cindy asked.

Watch understood. 'Time will begin to flow backwards. The effect of the necklaces on us might begin to reverse itself.'

'It's a possibility,' Adam said. 'I can't guarantee anything.'

'I say we try it,' Sally said. 'I think I'm going to be needing a nappy soon.'

'How sweet,' Cindy said.

'Don't joke,' Sally warned.

'This hourglass weighs a ton,' Mireen said. 'How will we turn it over?'

Watch flexed his muscles. 'No problem. I can lift it up with one hand.'

'But Mireen has a point,' Adam warned. 'If our

110

experiment works, we'll have to turn the hourglass back round. Then you won't be super-strong any more, Watch. We might get trapped in a time warp, where we have to live our lives backwards.'

'I refuse to go through all my psychological crises over again,' Sally said. 'I just finished with that junk.'

'We can worry about that problem when we come to it,' Watch said.

'I would rather worry about it now,' Adam said.

Watch did something unusual then. He reached out and touched Adam's shoulder. He held his friend's eye.

'Adam,' he said. 'A moment ago you said I had faith. That's why I wasn't hurt by my necklace. Well, I have faith now. If we do this, everything will work out. Ann Templeton will know we have passed our test. She will help us if we need help.'

'You really think so?' Adam asked. 'After all she's put us through, you still think she's a good witch?'

Watch didn't hesitate. 'I'm sure of it.'

'So am I,' Mireen added. 'She may be a witch to you, but she's still my mother. I trust her.'

'OK,' Adam said, putting his necklace back on. 'Let's do it. Let's see if we can't get ourselves back to normal.'

With the exception of Mireen, each of them put

their necklaces back on. Watch approached the glowing hourglass. He was as strong as he looked. In one smooth move, he inverted the magical time keeper.

Now the sparkling stardust began to flow *upwards*.

A wave of drowsiness swept over Adam. He blinked, trying to rub it from his eyes, but noticed he was not alone with his tired feelings. Each of them was slumping slowly to the ground. Now they really were in the witch's hands.

There was nothing Adam could do.

The drowsiness was too hard to resist.

He closed his eyes and blacked out.

Epilogue

That evening, while enjoying milk and doughnuts at their favourite coffee shop, they traded stories about what they experienced after the hourglass had been inverted. But basically all their stories were the same. They had fallen asleep and wakened outside beside the castle, in the same shape as when they entered the castle. They'd had another great adventure, but nothing had changed.

Or had it?

Mireen had not been with them when they had wakened.

'But maybe now her mother will let her come out and play sometimes,' Cindy said. 'I imagine Mireen will want to see us again.'

'I want to see her again,' Watch said quietly.

Sally shoved his side. 'You don't have a crush on her, do you, Watch?'

'No,' he said quickly.

'That would spoil your cool and detached image,' Adam teased.

Watch smiled to himself. '*She* didn't want to change my image too much.'

'Who is she?' Sally asked. 'What are you talking about?'

'Ann Templeton,' Watch said. 'She actually woke me before you guys, when we were still inside the castle. I don't know if she wants me to talk about it, but I guess it's all right.'

'What did she say to you?' Adam asked.

'Not much. She just told me to take off my necklace.'

They all jumped. 'Then you stopped the reversal process!' Cindy exclaimed. 'You can see without your glasses.' She paused. 'But you still have your glasses on.'

Watch nodded. 'I had reversed to almost how I was before I entered the castle. She told me that was for the best, for now. But she did allow my eyes to be improved enough that I won't have to keep bumping into things.'

'That's a miracle,' Cindy said. 'You must be grateful.'

114

'I am,' Watch said shyly.

'Wait a second,' Sally said. 'I would be angry with her. She could have at least wakened you early enough so that you didn't have to wear glasses at all. For that matter, she should have given you the necklace. She promised it to us if we passed the test. If anyone passed it, Watch, I think it was you.'

Watch smiled and shook his head. 'She said she didn't want to do that.'

'Why not?' Sally demanded.

'She said I looked better in glasses,' Watch said simply.

Sally thought for a moment, as she stared at her friend.

Then she too smiled. It was a happy smile.

'For once I agree with her,' Sally said.

If you've enjoyed these adventures, turn the page for the first chapter in Christopher Pike's next Spooksville chiller . . .

The Dark Corner

Look out for the next Spooksville story

The Little People

Strange visitors have come to Spooksville.

At first they play harmless tricks – but soon the tricks turn cruel, and Adam, Sally, Watch and Cindy are fighting for their lives.

Who are these little creatures? Why are they here? And how can Adam and his friends make them go away?

Spooksville

The Cold People

Why are there huge ice blocks in the forest near Spooksville? Adam and his friends are dying to know what's inside.

So they melt one – a big mistake.

A man steps out of the melting ice. He has cold eyes. An icy touch.

And he wants to turn all the inhabitants of Spooksville into Cold People. Can Adam and the others stop him?

More young spine-tinglers from Hodder Children's Books
Laugh till you scream with
Tom B. Stone's
GRAVEYARD SCHOOL series

❏	63693 9	Deadly Dinners	£2.99
❏	63694 7	The Headless Bike Rider	£2.99
❏	63600 9	Wicked Wheels	£2.99
❏	63601 7	Little Pet Werewolf	£2.99
❏	63602 5	Revenge of the Dinosaurs	£2.99
❏	63603 3	Camp Dracula	£2.99
❏	66476 2	Slime Lake	£2.99

All Hodder Children's books are available at your local bookshop or newsagent, or can be ordered direct from the publisher. Just tick the titles you want and fill in the form below. Prices and availability subject to change without notice.

Hodder Children's Books, Cash Sales Department, Bookpoint, 39 Milton Park, Abingdon, OXON, OX14 4TD, UK. If you have a credit card you may order by telephone – (01235) 400414.

Please enclose a cheque or postal order made payable to Bookpoint Ltd to the value of the cover price and allow the following for postage and packing:
UK & BFPO – £1.00 for the first book, 50p for the second book, and 30p for each additional book ordered up to a maximum charge of £3.00.
OVERSEAS & EIRE – £2.00 for the first book, £1.00 for the second book, and 50p for each additional book.

Name ....

Address ....

....

....

If you would prefer to pay by credit card, please complete:
Please debit my Visa/Access/Diner's Card/American Express (delete as applicable) card no:

Signature ....

ExpiryDate ....

Spooksville
CHRISTOPHER PIKE

❏	72415 3	The Secret Path	£3.50
❏	72416 1	The Howling Ghost	£3.50
❏	72417 X	The Haunted Cave	£3.50
❏	72437 4	The Wishing Stone	£3.50
❏	72438 2	The Wicked Cat	£3.50
❏	72439 0	The Deadly Past	£3.50
❏	72440 4	The Hidden Beast	£3.50

All Hodder Children's books are available at your local bookshop, or can be ordered direct from the publisher. Just tick the titles you would like and complete the details below. Prices and availability are subject to change without prior notice.

Please enclose a cheque or postal order made payable to *Bookpoint Ltd*, and send to: Hodder Children's Books, 39 Milton Park, Abingdon, OXON OX14 4TD, UK.
Email Address: orders@bookpoint.co.uk

If you would prefer to pay by credit card, our call centre team would be delighted to take your order by telephone. Our direct line *01235 400414* (lines open 9.00 am–6.00 pm Monday to Saturday, 24 hour message answering service). Alternatively you can send a fax on *01235 400454*.

TITLE	FIRST NAME	SURNAME	
ADDRESS			
DAYTIME TEL:		POST CODE	

If you would prefer to pay by credit card, please complete:
Please debit my Visa/Access/Diner's Card/American Express (delete as applicable) card no:

Signature ....

Expiry Date: ....

If you would NOT like to receive further information on our products please tick the box. ❏